Friends

for Life

Friends
for Life

a novel by Meg Wolitzer

Crown Publishers, Inc., New York

Published by Crown Publishers, Inc., 201 East 50th Street, New York, New York 10022. Member of the Crown Publishing Group.

Random House, Inc. New York, Toronto, London, Sydney, Auckland

CROWN is a trademark of Crown Publishers, Inc.

Manufactured in the U.S.A.

Design by Lauren Dong

Library of Congress Cataloging-in-Publication Data
Wolitzer, Meg.
    Friends for life : a novel / by Meg Wolitzer.—1st ed.
    p. cm.
    1. Women—New York (N.Y.)—Fiction. 2.
Friendship—New York (N.Y.)—Fiction. I. Title.
  PS3573.0564F75 1994
  813'.54—dc20   93-32353
                                            CIP

ISBN 0-517-59586-9

10 9 8 7 6 5 4 3 2 1

First Edition

For Martha Parker

The author would like to thank Nora Ephron,
who saw the possibilities in this story.
Also, many thanks to Betty A. Prashker,
Lynda Obst, and, as always, Peter Matson.

Part One

One

Three women in a restaurant: *what a cliché.* Three women huddling around the bread basket as though it were a campfire, nominally eating their scant suppers, ordering mammoth bottles of water as though suffering from a lengthy, tropical thirst. Three women who had performed poorly in math, but who now knew how to split a check so precisely that nobody ever underpaid, nobody overpaid, and everyone was happy. When you saw a table with three women around it, that was what you were supposed to think. But these three women were different, and they prided themselves on it. First of all, as they liked to tell people, they had known one another forever. They were not recent, fast friends, all working as buyers or lawyers, women who spoke a certain brand of brittle, inbred shoptalk that did not translate well when it escaped into the room at large. They had a *history* together, they would tell people, although sometimes the word seemed grandiose, as though the three of them had all been members of the French

Resistance, or quietly stoic army nurses during the Tet Offensive.

They met in the same restaurant for dinner on the first Monday of each month because it was what they had done for years; no one could remember who had suggested it first. Two of them disliked each other, and always had, but that didn't seem to matter. They were bound together for life, even though none of them had much in common anymore, except a history that took them back to the small, dull suburb where their parents still lived. In appearance, they were an odd collection of women—an assortment, one of each. Maybe because they were so different, when their voices made it past the invisible circle inscribed around their restaurant table, the things they said seemed so potentially interesting that passing waiters sometimes stopped, pretending to straighten a rose in some other table's bud vase, and listened.

Tonight Meredith arrived first, as always. When she walked through the door of the Lucky Wok, the only other people in the place were an elderly Chinese woman sitting behind the cash register doing the "Jumble" in the newspaper, and the owner of the restaurant, a slim man in a suit who showed Meredith to a table way in the back. Silently, seductively, he helped her remove her coat, lifting it by its scruff with his small, elegant hands, and lingering behind her for too long before spiriting it away.

Wherever she went, men paid unusual attention. Meredith Guzzi had a terrible name, and she knew it, but at twenty-eight she was a beautiful woman, which more than made up for the terrible name. Men were always making confessions to Meredith, telling her facts about themselves that they claimed they had told no one else. She had heard how a certain scar had come to be; how, as a child, another man had spied his mother writhing beneath the meter man. They gave her gifts, too, sometimes very expensive lingerie, smiling as they handed her the shallow boxes that seemed to hold only air.

Now Meredith took a novel from her purse and tried to read it as she sat waiting for Lisa and Ann to arrive. The book was *Middlemarch,* which she had been telling people was her favorite novel for years. She had vowed that she would finally read it, *really* read it, and this was as good a time as any to begin. *"Miss Brooke had that kind of beauty which seems to be thrown into relief by poor dress,"* she read, and the opening line seemed promising this time around, exciting her to the idea that later tonight, after she and Alan were done making love and he started pulling on his clothes to go home, instead of crying in bed for the rest of the night, she could prop herself up and read this book. All the lamentable details of her own life would leave her: the fact that she loved a man who wasn't free to stay the night with her, a man who was nearly twice her age. Instead, she would sink gratefully into the archaic customs and lingo of the nineteenth century. And, as a bonus, the next time she told someone that *Middlemarch* was her favorite novel, she would no longer be lying.

Meredith flexed the spine of the book so the pages lay pleasingly flat. But the lighting in this restaurant was weak, and there was Chinese music coming in through the speakers: nasal female bleating, accompanied by mandolin. *"Miss Brooke had that kind of beauty . . ."* she read again, squinting hard, and she knew it was hopeless. Suddenly, Lisa arrived at the table. She and Meredith exchanged double air-kisses in their professional, vaguely European way, then Lisa shrugged off her coat, revealing her white jacket with the beeper and hospital ID still clipped to the pocket. The laminated photograph showed a jaunty version of Lisa smiling at the photographer. The picture had been taken at the beginning of her internship, and apparently she hadn't yet known what she was getting into. Now she knew, all right. Lisa Vopilska was pretty in an anemic, undistinguished way, with straight blond hair that she had worn swept back in a headband ever since it had caught fire over a Bunsen burner during her first week of medical school. She was well-dressed and appealing, although if you looked closely, you saw that something was off. Her skin was too pale, sickly, like a minor character in *The Magic Mountain,* and her eyes looked crazy. Here was a woman who did not sleep.

"Listen," Meredith said right away. "I need to talk. Before Ann gets here." Lisa immediately looked concerned; she seemed about to reach over and start palpating the glands in Meredith's neck. "I'm in love," Meredith said. "But I can't tell you his name."

"He's a Kennedy," said Lisa. "Oh God, you're dating one of that new generation of Kennedys."

"Hardly," said Meredith. "Look, I'll tell you, but you must swear this will go no further. You cannot tell Ann. She'd walk around with it on a sandwich board."

"I swear," said Lisa, breathless.

Meredith leaned in close, and they looked like two women having a tryst in an out-of-the-way restaurant. From the front of the room, the owner watched them with interest. But suddenly the heavy front door swung open and cold air swept inside. "It's the Queen of Perfect Timing," said Meredith, and she sat back furiously in her chair as Ann Rogoff stamped in, dressed in a ballooning down coat. Her face was red and there was snow dotting being suspended in these sleeping bags forever. It was a relief to unravel their thoughts ahead to age thirty, and to know that even if they eventually became too unacceptable for any man to consider loving them, even if they never managed to complete the Darwinian climb out of adolescence and up onto the smooth rocks of everything that followed, they would still have one another. Of course, they all knew it wouldn't come to this; at least, it wouldn't come to this for Meredith. At twelve she was already a great beauty. Unlike the rest of them, Meredith had breasts; they pushed against her blouses, they announced themselves to the world, and their existence defeated the other three girls, who sat miserably, waiting to be claimed by their future bodies. Meredith had cheekbones, too, and hair that fell over one eye. She looked as though she really should consider taking up smoking at an early age; her fingers seemed to naturally separate, leaving a contoured space where a cigarette would fit. When the four girls trudged along the shadeless shoulder of the turnpike to eat at Burger Man—home of the triangular burger—teenaged boys driving by occasionally stopped the wide, boatlike American cars that belonged to their fathers, and asked if the girls wanted a ride. One time, a boy pointed from the window of a burgundy Seville, and said, "Just you. The pretty one." When they arrived at Burger Man that particular day, the four girls ate their triangles of meat and repeated their vows never to part, this time more fervently than usual. "The pretty one" had unwittingly made her debut, had been presented to the world at large, and there was nothing any of them could do about it.

To make matters worse, six months later, Barbara Krell's father was transferred to his company's Cincinnati branch office, and without warning Barbara was whisked away from them forever. At first, there was a rapid, melodramatic exchange of letters—the bottom of the stationery crawling with X's and O's—but after a while, Barbara began to write enthusiastically about some girl she had met named Doreen, who was double-jointed and who owned the largest collection of troll dolls Barbara had ever seen. After a while, the flurry of letters slowed, then stopped.

"What about our song?" Lisa said plaintively one Saturday night as the three remaining friends lay sadly in Ann's bedroom in the dark. "What about MerBaLisAn? What are we supposed to do when we come to the 'Ba'?" Ann suggested that they might hum, and Lisa tested this out. "Mer*hmm*LisAn," she tried. "Friends forever, Mer*hmm*LisAn." This new version sounded truly odd, but there was no other choice. Eventually they stopped talking and lay in silence, but they could not stop thinking about how one of their own had been torn from them, and how if that had happened, anything could. Life might continue picking them off one by one, calling them away into passionate love, or death, or Cincinnati. Trapped in the green nylon of the sleeping bags that Ann's father had bought at Wilderness World, and which had never been taken beyond the wilds of his daughter's bedroom, these girls longed to be plucked from their ordinary lives. They wanted to enter the world, they wanted to be in love.

Meredith had explained both love and sex to them in graphic and unsentimental detail. She had drawn a series of diagrams on index cards that were meant to be used for their project on Incan civilization. The back of one of the cards bore a crossed-out drawing of an Incan woman grinding cornmeal. If you flipped the card over, you could see Meredith's rendering of a man with a penis sticking straight out like a billy club, and a woman lying with her legs open—another part of Incan civilization. It was part of the entire *world,* and as the girls grew older, eventually they joined that world, were one by one initiated, taken to bed, outfitted with devices, some plastic, some metal, and now, at twenty-eight, very little was a surprise to them anymore.

"So how's *Middlemarch*?" Ann asked Meredith, nodding toward the thick book that now lay closed on the table. "Did you get to the part where she marries Casaubon?"

"No," said Meredith coldly. She took the book off the table and slipped it underneath her chair. This was aggression on Ann's part: a simple question that Lisa would barely notice, but which Meredith understood for all it was worth. Ann liked to remind Meredith that she had read everything, and Meredith had read nothing. At Yale, Ann had stayed up late into the night in the basement lounge of the library, swigging Diet Coke and reading German and French novels in their delicate yellow and red paper jackets, then stumbling back to her room in a cluster of other smart-mouthed women and their appreciative gay male friends.

Up at Brandeis, Meredith's own college experience had been dominated by her boyfriend, John Staley, a thick, handsome tree of a twenty-year-old, with whom she forgot that she had ever known how to read. Like other men, John was obsessed with Meredith, and he kept her a willing prisoner in his rancid dorm room, with his athletic jerseys flung over chairs, his overused, crusty water pipe on the bookshelf. They were both political science majors, and in fact had met in a small seminar on Lucretius, Hobbes, and Locke. One day after class, they went for a walk along campus, and John quoted from Lucretius in his impressively deep voice. " 'All nature as it is in itself consists of two things,' " he began. " 'Bodies and the vacant space in which the bodies are situated and through which they move in different directions.' By the way," he added, "here's where I play lacrosse. I really busted up my knee last year." His voice barely changed as he went from materialism to lacrosse. The sport sounded like the name of a lesser French philosopher, Meredith thought, and she and John joked about this in the following weeks. "As Lacrosse once said, in his 'Varsity Dialectics' . . ." she would say, but after a while, philosophy left their conversations completely, even all jokes about the subject, replaced by the far more wondrous subject of sex. On the lawn outside the window of John's room, Frisbees were flung, shanties were erected to demonstrate the plight of South Africa, but here, in John Staley's cubicle, Meredith and John tangled together on his sheets—two great-looking undergraduates who had found each other easily—the way great-looking people always do.

In the spring of her senior year, Meredith became pregnant. John said he wanted to go with her for the abortion, but she couldn't be sure whether he was telling the truth; his bass voice had a way of imbuing everything with a semblance of earnestness that often wasn't really there. Besides, she was depressed by the thought of his large, doglike face poking over her as she swam up from anesthesia on a cot in the nearby Susan B. Anthony Clinic. So she decided to ask Lisa to accompany her instead. Lisa was wonderful, bringing *Vogue* and red Twizzlers and simply sitting and holding Meredith's hand afterward.

The recovery room was populated by fifteen-year-old girls who looked as if they hadn't a clue as to how they had gotten here.

"Are you okay?" Lisa asked, her voice soft.

"Not terrible," said Meredith. "The Susan B. Anthony Clinic is a great place."

"But her coin really bombed," said Lisa, and Meredith was able to laugh a little, before she went back to sleep.

The next day Meredith broke up with John, and though she had been dreading the confrontation, he didn't seem all that surprised. They had begun to take each other's strong, handsome bodies for granted. They had grown bored in equal measure, so that the break-up was simple, to an almost embarrassing degree. It would have been better if he had objected a little more, or even if he had sat his one-hundred-ninety-pound lacrosse-playing body down on his bed and cried like a newborn. But he said he understood and he held her tenderly, and then she slipped from his room. Meredith spent her final semester at college trying desperately to learn something, so that the whole thing wouldn't have been a terrible waste, her parents' tens of thousands of dollars spent so that someone could perform hours of cunnilingus on their very responsive daughter.

Now, when Ann casually asked, "So how's *Middlemarch?*" the question was particularly cruel. Meredith knew it, and Ann knew it; only Lisa seemed unaware of subtext. At the University of Pennsylvania she had been sequestered in laboratories, dissecting dogs. Forced to read novels as part of her freshman English colloquium, she frantically telephoned Meredith and Ann and asked, "Do you think Anna Karenina had something wrong with her, I mean neurologically? In some cases of sexual compulsiveness, the brain registers a lack of some chemicals; I think it has to do with serotonin levels."

"Lisa dear," Meredith said patiently, "I love you more than life itself, but I have to tell you: she wasn't a real person."

"Yes, I *know* that," Lisa said, but she didn't know that, not really. She felt so bad for Anna Karenina, that if she could have, she would have thrown herself into the path of that oncoming train and pulled the poor, chemically unbalanced woman to safety.

"So get this," Ann was saying in the middle of the meal. "My mother wants me to schlepp out to her beauty salon and have my hair styled by someone named Mr. Leopold. So I say, 'Fine. And if he's not available, should I ask for Mr. Loeb?' So she gets all upset, and says how 'cute' I used to look when I had my hair styled like my friend Meredith Guzzi. She says I should find out who does your hair, Meredith. If I had my hair done like you, she says my dance card would be full."

"If you really want to meet a lot of men, you should go to medical school," said Lisa.

"Would I have to take math?"

"Not that you ever want to sleep with them," said Lisa.

"What about you, Meredith?" asked Ann. "Are you seeing someone?"

"I'm not free to talk about it," said Meredith.

"Oh, those pesky Pentagon rules."

"Really, Ann, it's no big deal," said Meredith.

"Since when is talking about men no big deal?" asked

Ann. "We've been talking about them forever."

"Except we used to call them boys," said Lisa. "Now all of a sudden they're men."

Ann burst into song. "I don't remember growing older/When . . . did . . . they?" As she sang, the waiter suddenly appeared, carrying a sizzling plate, which he placed in front of Meredith.

"For you, pretty lady," he said. "Jumbo crispy prawns, compliments of the owner."

"Here we go again," muttered Lisa. This had happened more than once before: a waiter bringing Meredith an appetizer, a drink, or something in flames, compliments of either the owner or a table of businessmen across the room. Now Meredith instructed him to remove the plate, but the waiter said the owner insisted, because Meredith was such a good customer and a lovely lady. Then he retreated, empty-handed, and the women sat in silence for a moment, the unwanted plate still hissing and spitting in front of them.

"You know, Lisa," Ann finally said, "you and I could sit here for a year, and no one would ever send free food over to us. We would have to get down on our knees and beg before anyone would even toss over a hunk of gristle. I swear, we might as well have bags over our heads. We might as well be lepers—"

"Thanks a lot," said Lisa.

"It's not easy when men are always looking at you," said Meredith. "When they always want a part of you. I happen to be having a hard time with a certain man in my life right now. It's a very delicate situation, because he's not only married, but he's famous." She paused, adding, "I wasn't going to say anything, because I get very emotional when I talk about Alan."

"Alan," Ann murmured. "Alan. Alan Funt? Alan Ludden? No, he's dead. Alan Ladd? Who *is* Alan Ladd?"

"Shane," said Lisa.

Suddenly Ann drew back. "Oh God, Meredith," she said. "Are you dating *Alan Alda*?"

"If you must know," said Meredith in a tired and noble voice, "it's Alan Seymour."

"Oh," said Ann.

"Oh," said Lisa.

Alan Seymour was the host of a public television show called "The Last Word." He was regarded as a left-wing William F. Buckley figure, and even resembled Buckley superficially, in that same gangly, praying mantis way. Ann was obviously disappointed at the disclosure. "Yeah, I've seen his show," she said mildly. "At least he doesn't say 'nucular.' I hate when they say 'nucular.' "

"I'm extremely unhappy," said Meredith, and she began to cry. At first her crying was a quiet matter, but after a moment she began sobbing in deep, searching gasps. She told them the whole story of how she and Alan had fallen in love when she went to work as a production assistant at the station. "We used to smile at each other in the elevator," she said, "and the second week I was working there, he took me out to lunch. So we're sitting in this restaurant, and we just start looking at each other. Here we are, talking about the topic for his next show— the plight of the boat people—and then he reaches over and holds my hand, and his hand is really big and soft, like a baseball glove. Then he says to me, 'Meredith, I am a married man and an honorable man, but I am so attracted to you that if I don't kiss you in the next five minutes, I think I will die.' " When she finished speaking, Lisa and Ann were left open-mouthed and silent. No man had ever said such things to either of them, and all signs seemed to indicate that no man ever would. "So now we're in love," Meredith continued. "And he'll never leave his wife, so we're kind of frozen like this forever."

"But what will you do?" asked Lisa.

"I have no idea."

"Meredith, who *does* do your hair?" Ann suddenly asked.

"What?" said Meredith. "No one. I do it myself."

"God does your hair, Meredith," said Ann. *"Mr. God."*

They left the Lucky Wok in a haze of Chinese spices, and it wasn't until they were out on the street, in the first shock of cold night air, that the spell of dinner and the palpable cloud of Meredith's unhappiness began to leave them. When the taxi deposited Meredith in front of her brownstone on West Seventy-eighth Street, she peered up and saw that the light in the window of her apartment was on, which meant that Alan was waiting. Meredith had given him a key this week. This gesture had probably been a mistake, but the moment had been so full of undiluted drama and promise that it had seemed worth it at the time. She had gone into Locks Plus on Tuesday and asked the sullen teenager behind the counter to make a copy of her Medeco key. Then she had waited in the tiny store, with its smells of metal and machine oil, surrounded by sample locks and keys that opened no door on earth, and as the teenager whirred away on his little key-making machine, she thought only about Alan. Then she rushed home to wait for him. "This is for you," she said when he arrived, holding the still-warm key out to him like a jewel.

Now Meredith hurried up the single steep flight and opened the door, and there was Alan, his six-foot-three frame lying unfolded on her too-short fold-out couch. He sprang up when she came in, as though afraid she was the police, or a reporter, or his wife. Alan was wearing only a big black waterproof watch and boxer shorts. Through the slit in his shorts she could see an intimation of his penis and a sprig of dark hair, which suddenly, depressingly, made her think of her father getting up to go pee on an early Sunday morning in her childhood. Meredith kissed Alan, and the kiss might have been prolonged, but then she saw him straighten out his arm and glance over at his watch.

"It's almost on!" he said, agitated, and he went to switch on the television, so she dutifully followed him to bed. The theme music had already started. "Good evening, and welcome to 'The Last Word,'" came the voice. "I'm your host, Alan Seymour." Beside her, Alan turned up the volume so that his big voice filled the tiny studio apartment.

As lovers, Meredith and Alan already had a fixed routine, like any other more mundane couple. He came to her apartment three nights a week, and depending on what time he got there, they either had sex before his show, or after his show. Never, never during. Watching the show with Alan was like going to an auction; if you even coughed, you were in trouble. Tonight the topic was international terrorism. The guests sat around the glazed oval maple table and sipped their water and fought like a dysfunctional family at dinner. Why weren't there any commercials on public television? Meredith needed to use the bathroom, but she didn't move. In the final moments of the show, Alan thanked his guests, then swiveled smartly toward the camera and said, "I'm Alan Seymour, and that's . . . 'The Last Word.' " The theme music was cranked up again, and Meredith shut off the set and darted to the toilet.

"You were good," she said through the closed door.

"Don't you think I look old?" he asked. "I'm fifty-four."

"My father's fifty-four," said Meredith. She finished up, then came out of the bathroom and got back into bed.

"Oh, God," said Alan. He grabbed a hand mirror from the night table and peered into it, scavenging for ruin.

"See, my point is that fifty-four seems young," Meredith said. "My father is very active. He and my mother go folk-dancing; you should see them. She wears a dirndl."

"Do you think I look like Adolphe Menjou?" he asked.

"*Who?*" said Meredith.

"Oh, forget it," said Alan, and he sighed.

She moved closer so that she could see into the small mirror, too. "Look at these lines around my eyes," she said. The mirror was an antique, and its thick circle of glass had a dull, speckly quality to it that made Meredith wonder about the mirror's original owner: some Victorian wife in a high collar, staring unhappily at the lines around her own mouth, too vain to worry about the real truth of the matter, that someday these imperfections wouldn't even exist, that her bones would be eroded down to the finest shavings, and that some new, vain young woman would be fretting over the same pointless concerns as she stared into the round hand mirror she had bought at a flea market on Columbus Avenue.

Now Alan and Meredith stared at their reflections together, with the same rapt attention they gave to watching "The Last Word." Finally Alan turned to her and said,

"What are we doing? I have to be home in two hours." He placed the mirror facedown on the night table and pulled her over so that she lay on top of him. He was hers for the next hour and three-quarters. She wanted to cry at the unfairness of all this, but his hands were stroking her long back, and she rose up slowly above him, almost against her will. Sex made everyone stupid, she thought. You know exactly what's going to happen, you can see the whole tragic story from start to finish, and yet all it takes is someone's oversized hands landing on your breasts and you become a happy idiot, a strapping, smiling milk maid in an operetta, singing as she goes about her business. *Fa la la, I'm in love with a married man. Fa la la, I'm throwing my life away. Fa la la la la . . .*

It wasn't until later, after Alan had pulled on his clothes and left, that Meredith realized she had left her copy of *Middlemarch* beneath her chair in the Chinese restaurant.

"She could have any man on earth," Lisa said when Ann answered the phone, "and she picks him."

"He's so old," said Ann. "And he's so . . . dry. Boring, even. Did you ever watch that show? It puts you right to sleep. A bunch of bitter people sitting around and discussing fiscal strategies or euthanasia. Meredith has gone out with plenty of men, but I tell you, I just do not understand this one."

"I guess we'll just have to accept the fact that she's really in love with him," said Lisa.

"Meredith is not capable of love. Total self-absorption, yes. Love, no."

"You are so hard on her, Ann. I'd love to hear what you two say about me when I'm not around."

"You know we don't speak when you're not around. If you dropped dead tomorrow, we'd never see each other again."

"Please, don't rush me."

"Except at your funeral, where she would completely hog the spotlight: 'Ode to Lisa,' by Meredith Guzzi: 'As I place a rose on thy grave/I think how the years will soon fade my beauty/O Lisa, I cry not for you, but for myself.' "

"You're terrible, Ann."

"And you love it."

A beep was heard. "That's my Call Waiting," said Lisa, and she clicked the button once and said hello.

"Are you on the other line with her?" Meredith asked.

"Don't say 'her,' " said Lisa.

"You sound like my father," said Meredith. "Don't call

your mother 'her.' Now, what is wrong with saying 'her'? I have never understood this."

"Look, let me call you back," said Lisa.

"Are you two talking about me?" asked Meredith.

Lisa paused, deciding. "No," she said. Meredith said good-bye. Lisa clicked the button again, and Ann resurfaced.

"Was that her?" asked Ann.

"Her? Yes, it was her. She asked if we were talking about her, and I said no. God, I feel so guilty."

"Lisa, don't you know by now that it's perfectly kosher for us to talk about each other? Nothing we say will ever be repeated. It's completely safe. In fact, it's very healthy."

"Oh?" said Lisa skeptically. "Healthy how?"

"You see, when two good friends talk about the third friend, it's like having a therapist, which I would otherwise never be able to afford, unless it was one of those free ones who advertise in the back of the *Village Voice* and hook you up to electrodes—"

"But she's our *friend*," said Lisa.

"So? I'm sure that you and Meredith talk about me. Am I right?"

"Well, sometimes," said Lisa. "And you don't mind?"

"What I don't know can't hurt me," Ann said piously.

"That's very mature of you."

"Just tell me the general theme," said Ann. "Is it my hair? My clothes? Or just, you know, my whole personality?"

"I'm hanging up now, Ann," said Lisa. "Good night."

21

Two

The first time she saw a cadaver, Lisa Vopilska desperately tried to remember what it had been like to play with dolls. If she could think of this dead person as a kind of huge doll, and have the freedom to manipulate the arms and legs the way she had done as a child, then maybe it wouldn't be so terrible, and maybe she wouldn't faint. Her partner in anatomy class didn't even blink when the body was revealed, but simply picked up the silver tools from where they lay, like someone poised before beginning lunch in an expensive restaurant. *Doll,* Lisa kept thinking, *pretend this is a doll,* but she had never in her childhood played with a doll made to look like a fifty-year-old man, a doll with a crop of coarse gray chest hair and fingernails as blue as sky. A doll who had dropped dead of a heart attack on Fifth Avenue, while wolfing down a two-dollar shish kebab. Lisa patted the sweat from her forehead. Dark rings began to appear at the edges of her vision, and eventually she had to sit down and put her head between her knees.

"Are you okay?" her partner asked, but he couldn't disguise his annoyance. Some doctor he would make.

"I just felt a little funny, that's all," Lisa explained. "You see, I'm trying to make the cadaver look like a doll."

Her partner had never played with a doll in his life; he had probably played with scalpels and clamps and autoclaves. "Come on, we'd better get started," he said flatly. Lisa took a breath, her lungs filling with pickling fumes. For a moment, she imagined having a nervous breakdown right here in the middle of the hushed, brightly lit lab. This was the medical school equivalent of those fantasies in which you stood during a quiet section of an orchestral performance at Carnegie Hall and started screaming "Fuck!" and "Shit!" as loud as you could. Nobody ever really had a breakdown at Carnegie Hall. The audience always sat docilely in their seats, listening or lightly dozing. And no one ever broke down during anatomy lab. This was the ring of fire you had to walk through if you wanted to become a doctor; there was no other way to get there. So Lisa shakily stood, then picked up a large knife, her partner steadying her hand. Together they began sawing into their cadaver, like newlyweds cutting the cake for a photo op.

Now, years later, Lisa Vopilska had become a well-respected medical resident who was often, to her dismay, called upon during rounds. She always tried to make herself appear as inconspicuous as possible during these moments, hoping that her pale hair and skin would help her fade into the phalanx of white coats. But the chief of staff admired her for some unknown reason and often singled her out. This morning he nodded in her direction and said, "Dr. Vopilska, will you examine the patient?"

The patient in question was a ninety-year-old black

woman named Mrs. Blondine Dixon. She lay in her bed hooked up to an IV and a monitor, surrounded by the bland, adolescent faces of medical students and recent doctors. Mrs. Dixon was cheerful and blithe, as though being visited by a circle of Christmas carolers.

"Mrs. Dixon," said Lisa, stepping forward and taking the woman's hand, "have you been experiencing any chest pains?"

"What's that, honey?"

"Chest pains? In your chest?" asked Lisa tenderly. She put her own hand over her heart. She hated asking questions; each one felt somehow like a violation, as though she were asking this woman to describe the most private, vulnerable moments of her long life, rather than the rudimentary details of breathing and living. Lisa knew that she could never have become a psychiatrist; during her psych rotation, she had had to force herself to sit at the intake table asking those poor, troubled people questions about their fantasies and sexual preferences. Even when a patient answered her questions willingly, Lisa felt like a cop in a *noir* film, interrogating a criminal under a circle of lamplight.

She repeated her question to Mrs. Dixon. "Chest pains?"

The woman smiled up at her. "Oh yes," she said.

Lisa glanced down at the chart, quickly searching for clues to disease. "How are you feeling today, Mrs. Dixon?" she asked.

"Fine, fine," said the woman.

Now Lisa lifted Mrs. Dixon's wrist; her pulse was fast and faint, like the pulse of a household pet. "Mrs. Dixon, have you had any difficulty breathing?" Lisa asked.

"How's that?"

"Does it hurt when you breathe?" said Lisa.

Mrs. Dixon stared at Lisa as though she'd just really begun to notice her, and then she smiled inappropriately. "We had just got ourselves married," she said, "and we had an apartment. Five rooms! My mother-in-law came and stayed for a month after the first child was born. She was a great help to me, a great help."

And all Lisa could do was smile helplessly back, listening to the whole story.

Later, one of the other residents fell into step beside her in the hall. Eric Zinn had always struck her as the kind of man who had been hyperactive as a boy, wearing a crash helmet as he tore around the living room, until eventually the energy got funneled into overachievement: Westinghouse Science Competition finalist, National Merit Scholar, M.I.T., Albert Einstein Medical College. Eric was handsome in that dark, bearded way that seemed kind of a cheat. Who knew how handsome he would really look without the facial hair that was as carefully maintained as topiary.

"Lisa?" he said. "You were really good in there. The patients love you. You're like their granddaughter."

"Thanks," Lisa said, pleased.

"I like watching you," he went on. "See, I come from this family of dermatologists. They're just waiting for me to join them, but how can I? I've always wanted to do big things with my life. Did you ever see *Fantastic Voyage*?" Lisa said she wasn't sure. "It takes place in the future," Eric continued. "Raquel Welch plays a surgeon, and she becomes really tiny so she and this team of surgeons can go inside a dying man's body and operate. They actually walk through the veins, which are like these long, dark tunnels, and finally they get to the heart, which is pounding so hard it's like an earthquake. When I was nine, it was my favorite movie. That's what I thought medicine would be like: exciting. You know, a voyage."

"Well, it can be," said Lisa.

"Not for my relatives," said Eric. "They all live in Wilmington, Delaware, and they have a monopoly on skin. We have this little saying in my family: 'If you have a wart, call Uncle Mort. If you have a mole, call Uncle Joel.' "

"And if you have psoriasis?" Lisa asked, and they both laughed. She felt the beginnings of heat moving around the border of her scalp and suddenly, absurdly, she imagined him kissing her. She realized that she could barely remember the last time she had been kissed. It had been during medical school, that much she knew, and the kisser had been another student. They had gone to his apartment and started the preliminaries for sex, but they had both smelled so strongly of formaldehyde that they decided to just give the whole thing up and get a pizza. After that thwarted experience, Lisa had mostly forgotten about sex, and had instead buried herself inside *Gray's Anatomy*. The body, in her view, became a collection of parts, swarming with disease. Who would actually want to kiss or, worse, *lick* any of those things? Being a doctor took a lot of the pleasure out of sex, and she imagined that sex between two doctors would be like an extremely thorough physical.

Over the course of three weeks, Lisa and Eric flirted energetically in the ratty faculty lounge and the doctors' cafeteria, and even in the predawn hell of the knife and gun club. One night, when they were both on call and the floor was surprisingly quiet, Eric came unannounced to Lisa's cubicle, where she lay sleeping. "It's me," he whispered through the door, and she groggily let him in. No one had seen him; he had slipped past the nurses, past three interns playing stud poker, and now here he was, right beside her. Lisa was in her green scrubs, which were creased from sleep. She thought how ugly she must look now, and how asexual. In her experience, men tended to like women who wore clothes that didn't have PROPERTY OF N.Y. HOSPITAL stamped all over them. But still, Eric moved closer and kissed her mouth, and within a minute he was lying on top of her, and they were both breathing hard.

Although she hadn't had sex in so long, it all came back to her in their fumblings, as though she were tasting a nostalgic food from her childhood: Ovaltine, Maypo. *Oh, yeah,* she thought. *Now I remember.* Eric was an unusually neat lover; he had folded his clothes over her chair before he climbed onto the cot, and he didn't even seem to sweat, unlike one man Lisa had gone to bed with in college, David Casselman, who had turned her bed into a Marimekko swamp. Eric pushed his penis inside, and then paused so they both could look at each other in that sheepish, pleased way that people do when they have sex with each other for the first time.

"Hi, you," he said.

"Hi, you," she answered.

"Are you okay?" he asked her. She didn't know what this question meant. Was he worried that he was somehow hurting her? It was a polite question, she decided, and its origins lay in the fact that Eric often inserted tubes down people's noses and throats.

"I'm fine," she whispered. He began to kiss her neck,

and Lisa thought again how much fun this was. Then his beeper went off.

Within a month Eric Zinn, M.D., was installed in Lisa's life, along with his rowing machine. Because he spent most nights at her apartment, he had lugged the thing over, scraping it along the three blocks between their buildings, and it now took up an inordinate amount of space in her living room. Before Eric, Lisa had been proud of what she had done with her apartment; she thought she had cleverly added a touch of Vermont Farmhouse to high-rise hospital housing. There was an antique friendship quilt on the bed, which had been made by a quilting bee in the 1880s, and all the women had signed their names in stitches: *Mabel Lennox,* she read. *Birdie Ames.* These were women who had sat contentedly each week among dozens of squares of material, and who had all long ago been buried in the earth of a Vermont graveyard, their headstones partially obscured by a quilting of green moss. On her walls, Lisa had hung a series of framed museum posters. "The Vopilska Collection," Ann called it. There was a Manet, and a Georgia O'Keeffe, and the mandatory David Hockney swimming pool. But now Eric's rowing machine was planted squarely against the far wall in the living room, a few feet to the left of a Diane Arbus poster of a dwarf. Every morning at six A.M. Eric worked the oars of his machine as he listened to Bruce Springsteen, whom he buoyantly referred to as "Bruce!" as though the two of them had been strapping and soulful Jersey drinking buddies.

Meredith and Ann hadn't yet met Eric. Soon, soon, Lisa promised them, but the idea of an introduction dinner made her sick with anxiety. Eric was different from all of them. He didn't like to sit and eat peanut M&M's and talk for hours; he didn't like to deconstruct "The Patty Duke Show" theme song. (Ann insisted that the lyrics "But Patty loves to rock and roll/The hot dog makes her lose control" overtly employed phallic imagery to show ur-"Patty" as an emerging sexual entity.) Eric was impatient and overzealous; sometimes his nervous leg-jiggling made him seem like a one-man band. Lisa wasn't comfortable with him in the way she was with Meredith and Ann, but she told herself that this was because of sexual tension. When sexual tension existed, you forced yourself to shave your legs, even in winter. You finally threw out the underwear with the unraveling elastic waistband. You refrained from dotting your face with Acne-Gone before bed. You replaced the thin lozenge of soap in your bathroom with a wicker basket of fragrant soap in the shapes of fruit. When sexual tension existed, you felt that you were on a mission. You made your body and your apartment and your whole life inviting.

As Lisa walked down York Avenue holding hands with Eric, she felt the smug relief of being young and attached and in love. Because of this status, at dinner in restaurants she was free to reach up and sweep the hair out of Eric's eyes. She could be frank with him about the ugly brown college sweatshirt he was wearing. And, best of all, they fucked all the time. She liked to use that word when she thought of sex with Eric; it made her feel adult and unembarrassed. It made her feel capable, even more so than the fact that the initials "M.D." were appended to her name.

At night Eric waited in her bed, happy as a pasha with the remote control in his hand, clicking the TV through its entire round of channels, as Lisa struggled with her diaphragm in the grim flicker of her bathroom light. One night in the bathroom, the diaphragm sprang from her hand and bounced off the tiled wall, slowly circling like a spinning coin, before settling down, once and for all, behind the toilet. She had to poke it out with the end of a toilet plunger, as though playing miniature hockey. She made a note to tell Meredith and Ann about this the next day; it would be added to their pantheon of anecdotes. Lisa and the Runaway Diaphragm—that sounded like the title of a children's book, she thought, starting to laugh as she rinsed the thing off in the sink.

"Is everything all right in there?" Eric called.

"Fine," Lisa said, coming out of the bathroom and climbing back into bed without another word.

"So we have to meet the mysterious Eric already," Ann said one night on the telephone. She had said this before.

"You will," Lisa promised again.

"What's the matter, is he homely or something?" said Ann. "A yellow tooth?"

"No, he's not homely," said Lisa. "He's very handsome." There was a long silence, and she realized that she sounded foolish, holding out like this. Why not let them meet him? So Lisa agreed to give a little party, and now Ann was planning on bringing somebody from the publishing house where she worked, and with whom she had slept the week before. Meredith could not bring Alan, of course, because he would not go out in public with her, or even attend a small dinner that might possibly link his name with hers. Instead, Meredith announced that she would bring the guacamole. On Saturday night, Lisa's best friends in the world would be meeting the man she loved, all of them gathering in her living room, under the dwarf.

Eric could not grasp the depth of her anxiety. On Saturday she hung the rug out on the tiny terrace and scoured the inside of the toaster oven with a tooth-brush. "They're going to look inside your toaster oven?" he asked.

"No," she said. "I don't even know what I'm doing. I'm losing my mind here."

"Just relax. It wasn't a big deal when you met Mitchell and Kevin, was it?" he asked her.

Mitchell and Kevin had been Eric's best friends as undergraduates. The friendship seemed to be wordless, as though they'd met at that deaf college, and not at M.I.T. When the three men got together, all they seemed to do was eat take-out chicken wings, drink beer, and watch the sports channel. Lisa hadn't even known that Eric liked sports. He'd never once discussed the subject with her. She knew him only in the context of the hospital or a restaurant or the bedroom; he was a good doctor, a good date, a good lover. He had no life for her outside those limited spheres.

His friend Mitchell lived in Philadelphia, and Kevin lived in Chicago, but one weekend in November the men convened in New York, sleeping on the floor of Lisa's apartment. All night, these three college friends, who had not been in the same room together for over a year, sat rapturous in the light of the television, watching a Rangers game, occasionally lifting bottles of Molson ale to their lips. Didn't they want to *talk*? she wondered. They hadn't seen each other in so long, and yet they all turned to face in the same direction, not saying a word, except to urge the Rangers' goalie to watch his ass. At the end of the weekend Eric, Mitchell, and Kevin hugged one another hard, as though in their silence they'd managed to transmit many profound and moving secrets. Maybe Eric imagined that Lisa's dinner would be a replay of the weekend with Mitchell and Kevin, except this time the women friends would all sit in front of the TV drinking white wine spritzers and watching figure skating.

Lisa not only wanted Eric to know everything about Lisa and Meredith, she also wanted him to love them unconditionally. She wanted the evening to end in a festival of love, everyone pulling on their coats while giving elaborate nods and winks of approval. At seven o'clock, Lisa stood terrified at the stove, poking around in a pan of chicken *marbella* and drinking wine from an old Flintstones jelly jar, and she wished she could stand like this all night, cooking the chicken into blackened submission, and slowly getting tanked.

"You want me to?" Eric asked when the buzzer honked, and she nodded gratefully. He went to the door and brought Meredith in. She looked wonderful, of course, with a forest-green scarf done in some elaborate knot at her throat, and her hair full and perfumey. When she came through the saloon doors of the kitchen to say hello, Eric was right behind her, so there was no time for a quick first-impression summit with either of them. Then the buzzer rang again, and Ann and David appeared. David Marcus was rather good-looking, although, like Ann, he sported a strange, almost tribal haircut. He and Ann were roughly the same size, and both of them wore shapeless black clothes that seemed cut from parachute silk. A small gypsy hoop adorned David's left earlobe, giving him that androgynous look that had begun to change the landscape of urban men. Ann seemed happy, lightly touching David and whispering cozily with him, as though they had been married for years. Eric marched back and forth to the closet with everybody's coats, and the dinner party began.

For the first half hour, they all sat around the coffee table, talking about the shockingly high incidence of guns in the schools, and discreetly spitting olive pits into napkins. Then Lisa went into the kitchen to fetch dinner. She bent down to the oven to retrieve the potatoes, and the blast of heat struck her full-face. She thought: *I don't want to go back out there. Let me die here like Sylvia Plath.* Then she noticed that the oven needed cleaning, and made a mental note to buy Easy-Off tomorrow. When she returned to the living room, the food was dispensed, and a long, knobby baguette got passed from hand to hand like a peace pipe. Billie Holiday sang "Strange Fruit" on the CD player, and at one point during the meal, everyone seemed to be chewing silently, not really talking. That sad, weary voice came through the speakers, singing her song about lynching, while the five white people sat eating chicken *marbella* and listening.

"I love this record," said Ann. "Billie Holiday was so tragic."

"What do you mean?" Eric asked.

Ann studied him for a second. "Well, she had a terrible life," she said. "And, you know, she died of a drug overdose. They found her like *this.*" Ann flopped heavily against the couch, one pale, bare arm flung out, her eyes open in a death stare. After a moment, David tapped her shoulder.

"You can wake up now, Lady Day," he said. "We've

brought you to the Betty Ford Clinic, and you're going to be just fine."

Ann sat up and continued eating. Eric looked bewildered, so Meredith turned to him and said, "Didn't you see *Lady Sings the Blues*?"

"No," said Eric.

Ann and Meredith just stared at him.

"You *didn't* see *Lady Sings the Blues*?" said Ann. "How is that possible?" She turned to David, who was innocently eating. "You saw it, didn't you?" she asked. He nodded and tried to say "Sure," but his mouth was filled with bread.

"What is it, a movie?" asked Eric, and Ann and Meredith now seemed ready to tug at their hair in disbelief. How could he not have seen this movie? they were thinking. How was it humanly possible? Lisa realized that it was time for her to intervene.

"Eric loves movies," she began nervously. "His favorite is that one where Raquel Welch gets really tiny—"

"Lisa," Eric interrupted, "I was nine."

"*Lady Sings the Blues*," said Meredith in a lofty voice, "is an extremely bad, extremely tragic movie."

"Well, as a physician, believe me, I've witnessed real tragedy," said Eric. "Newborn babies with their hearts outside their bodies, just *dangling* there—"

Throughout what was left of the evening, Eric continued to tell tales of medical drama. During the salad course, he told a story from his gastroenterology rotation: ". . . and by the time we got him into surgery," he said, "his stomach had actually *exploded*." During the entree, Eric was still going strong: ". . . so her brain," he said, "was so filled with fluid that the head was like a *watermelon*."

35

Lisa watched the three others recoil as though they were one unified bloc of squeamishness. Later, when the plates were being cleared, she went back through the saloon doors into the kitchen, where Ann and Meredith were standing, talking in a manner that actually seemed intimate.

They turned and told her that they thought Eric was great. They also said that he was handsome, which of course was indisputably true, and they said that his medical stories were very moving. Lisa hugged them hard and in that moment she felt like bursting into tears, because it finally seemed to her that she could have it all, that she didn't have to choose, that those inspirational books for women, written by peppy female Ph.D's with smart haircuts were actually true, and she could keep everyone she loved all around her in one big communal huddle.

The rest of the evening was unmemorable, but Lisa took extraordinary pleasure from the fact that nothing terrible happened. No one insulted anyone else. There were no horrible moments of embarrassment, no big Black Holes of mortification into which Lisa longed to jump. The evening maintained a steady, bearable rhythm, although it wasn't one of those wonderful nights where Meredith, Lisa, and Ann talked and talked, their words overlapping, their entire conversation forged in the exhilarated code of old friends.

But all night long, Eric seemed stunted by the overwhelming force that was MerLisAn. David could fend for himself, but not Eric. How could Eric ever compete with this massive wall of women? Finally the meal was over and Billie Holiday had stopped singing, and pretty soon someone would make the first move toward going home. Lisa looked around the room at the last gasps of this dinner party, noticing the way Eric was slumped slightly against the couch, his arms folded against his chest as though protecting himself against expected blows, and the way Meredith and Ann seemed to triumphantly rise up on either side of him like the Furies. Poor Eric, was all Lisa could think. Poor, poor Eric. What had he gotten himself into?

Later, lying beside him in the dark, facing him as she always did, so that she could fall asleep to the soft metronome of his breathing, she asked him, "So you think it went okay?"

"I told you, honey, yes," he said.

"You really liked them? Would they pass the train test?"

"The what?" asked Eric.

"If you were on a train and they walked down the aisle, would you hope they sat next to you, or would you want them to sit somewhere else?" This was a test that Meredith, Lisa, and Ann had devised years before, to rate various people they met, whether as potential friends or lovers.

Eric squinted. "Is it a very long trip?" he asked. "I usually like to read."

"You're so literal!" said Lisa.

"Actually, I don't think they would want to sit with me," he said, and Lisa insisted that that wasn't true.

"In fact," she said, "they said you were moving."

"Moving? Really?" said Eric. "Even though I've never seen *Lady Sings the Blues*? You'd think I said I kidnapped the Lindbergh baby."

Toward the end of dinner, Meredith and Ann had whispered frantically to each other in Lisa's kitchen. "What is she thinking of?" Ann hissed. "Could you die?"

"It won't last," said Meredith. "It's obviously a sexual thing. Lisa's never had that before. She's spent her whole life in laboratories doing things with Petri dishes, and going totally unnoticed, and finally here's somebody who chose her, and it makes her feel special."

"Any second now," said Ann, "she's going to walk through those swinging doors, and she's going to look at us with those Bambi eyes, and she's going to want to know what we think. You're the one who says we should be nice. So you come up with an adjective. Anything."

"What is this, Mad Libs?" asked Meredith.

"I'm serious!" said Ann. "Come on!"

"Moving," Meredith said. "We can tell her we thought he was moving."

"Who's going to believe that?" asked Ann. "Oh, come on, Meredith, we can do better than that. Think!"

Suddenly the saloon doors swung open and Lisa marched in with the rest of the plates. "Ann," she said, "I think David is so great."

"Oh, thanks," said Ann. "I mean, I had nothing to do with his being great, but thanks anyway."

There was an endless pause. Ann added, almost mournfully, "I think Eric is great, too."

"He really is, Lisa," said Meredith.

"Really?" Lisa asked.

"Oh yeah," said Ann. "He's so good-looking. And the

way he talked about medicine, it was extremely . . . moving."

"You guys are terrific," said Lisa. "I started worrying that things weren't going well, but I guess it's just me, Lisa the Paranoid."

"Oh, definitely," said Meredith.

Lisa hugged both of them roughly and quickly, then went back out into the living room. The doors swung a few times behind her, giving glimpses of Eric, who sat innocent of all this, waiting for dessert. Meredith and Ann looked at each other with the weary, damning look of coconspirators, who were now joined together for the long run.

Three

The year Ann saw *The Sound of Music,* she desperately wanted to be a nun. Her mother had to remind her over and over that she could not become a nun because she was Jewish. "Oh yeah," Ann always said. "I forgot." The power of her longing was greater than logic, and besides, she didn't really grasp the negative connection between being Jewish and being a nun, although she pretended she did. All Ann Rogoff knew was that being a nun meant you could live on a mountain with a gaggle of other nuns, at an Olympian remove from pollution and traffic and the daily problems of ordinary human beings. You and your "sisters" would all wear simple black and white—easy on the eyes—and you would sit in a circle, gently praying or singing an intricately harmonized version of "Amazing Grace." When the weather was clement, you could wander the vast convent grounds, picking berries and gathering wildflowers as a special gift for the Mother Superior. You could live the life that Julie Andrews had lived at the beginning of *The Sound of Music,* before she had inexplicably thrown it away to babysit for all those Trapps. Ann wanted to be back on that mountain with Julie Andrews, who was extremely beautiful—almost handsome—and had a crystalline singing voice. The harmonies of "Amazing Grace" would never faze Julie; she was the one whose voice could rise above the others, where it could be easily heard by God.

Ann dwelled on this fantasy a great deal as a little girl, lining up her dolls and adjusting the limbs of the bendable ones, so they looked as though they were kneeling on prayer stools. Once she even shaved Chatty Cathy's head with her mother's Lady Schick razor, as the doll belonged to a particularly strict order.

While it wasn't surprising that Ann had never become a nun, she hadn't really become much of a Jew, either. Over the years since her bat mitzvah she had lapsed into a vague, softheaded kind of Jewishness that involved *thinking* about fasting during the high holidays, then at the last minute changing her mind and microwaving a frozen burrito. But she was the only Jew among MerLisAn, and felt she ought to at least pretend a greater attachment to her faith in order to set a good example.

Ann currently spent her days at Eberhardt Publishers, where she sat on one side of a divider, reading manuscripts and typing up letters for the young, fussy editor she worked for, whose name was Harry Corning, and who, despite his British accent and supposed expertise in the works of Laurence Sterne, had truly dumb taste in current fiction. He often lightly slapped manuscripts down on Ann's desk and murmured, "Tell me what you think of this." The novels tended to be flat and creepy: *I'm staying up all night and feeling wired, so I eat a pack of Ho-hos and a can of Orange Crush. I like the name Crush. It reminds me* her that these writers led cushy lives of winning grants and giving readings and sleeping late, while Ann, who had a degree in English Literature from Yale—with honors!—made fifteen thousand a year in a job where no one noticed her or praised her, and where the wall of her office didn't even reach all the way up to the ceiling.

Now, as she sat reading, she felt something land in her hair. She looked up, and saw that paper clips were being lobbed at her from the other side of the divider, where David Marcus sat. He had become the one bright spot here for her at Eberhardt. David was the editorial assistant for a motherly editor named Helen Warren, whose specialty was books about gardening and home improvement. In this vast publishing house, with its background noise of computer keyboards and the infertility-inducing hum of fluorescent lights, David was her one real friend and, recently, her lover. He was writing a novel in his spare time, a coming-of-age story about a young, lonely man who moves to New York and gets a job in publishing. For the first several months that they had shared a wall, she had assumed he was gay, largely because of the earring in his ear and the fact that he actually seemed nice.

But during one memorable lunch hour, he had declared his sexual feelings toward her. They had been at a street fair, a fair exactly like every other one in New York, with rings of dough frying in vats of rancid oil, children sucking on ices that turned their mouths drowning-victim-blue, grown men with ribbed, sleeveless undershirts and hairy arms, squinting into the range-finders of air rifles and shooting off the heads of tin ducks so they could win pink acrylic monkeys for the special ladies in their lives. Ann and David shuffled through the crowd, muttering predictable, sarcastic, elitist comments to each other, and then they stopped to have their blood pressure taken at the goody-goody Red Cross booth in the midst of this trashy festival. David's pressure was surprisingly high, and when the volunteer asked if medical procedures usually made him nervous, he said no, it wasn't that, and then turned to Ann with soulful eyes. Me? she'd said to him. Me? *I* make you nervous? He nodded yes, and then he tried to take her hand in his, but their arms were kept apart by the blood pressure cuffs, like prisoners on a chain-gang.

She looked across the table at the Red Cross booth and wondered if she was attracted to him, too. She had almost never, in her life, experienced that singular, sickening thud of arousal that Meredith often described when talking about men. But no one was quite like Meredith, whose knowledge of sex seemed to be so complete that she could play the sex category on "Jeopardy" opposite Masters and Johnson, and win. Meredith owned a set of ben-wa balls that had been given to her by a man named Phillip who had been to the Orient on a Luce Fellowship, and had bought them in bulk. Meredith had experienced the subtle pleasures of tantric sex. She knew that the tiny hole on the end of a man's penis was called a meatus. Meredith knew everything, and when David announced his attraction to Ann, she wished Meredith were here, living inside her body, so that she could tell her whether Ann's feelings constituted authentic sexual desire. Is this *it*? she wanted to know. She certainly liked David, but there wasn't any obvious imperative to eroticize this friendship. Until this very moment, she and David had been the most comfortable of friends. Little notes passed through the seam in their wall divider, and paper clips rained down on her head. She worried at first that if they became lovers, all of that would end, replaced by new, moony looks as David peered down at her, and occasional vases of freesia left on her desk. Something was already starting to spoil; she could feel it happen, the silent wreckage of a good friendship, and this reminded her of her mother, who would eye a dish of mayonnaise left out on a picnic table during a family barbecue, as though convinced she could sense the exact moment when it would start to turn.

His head appeared now, the sincere face, the antique eyeglasses and wispy hair—a young man who still mooned over Hendrix and the Weather Underground and People's Park, even though he had pretty much missed the whole thing when it was happening. "Want to get lunch?" David asked. Ann got her coat and they headed for the Three Cousins coffee shop around the corner. On the way, they passed by the restaurant Gepetto, just as Harry Corning was going inside with the literary agent Evan Bright. The heavy door was open wide enough to reveal a few yards of the warm, pale insides of the four-star restaurant. Harry usually returned from lunch at three o'clock, in a woozy, sated condition, the corners of his mouth still shiny with olive oil, humming whatever music had been piped into his restaurant that day, and punctuating the humming with a few discreet, satisfied belches. Usually, whenever Ann saw Harry entering a restaurant with one of his publishing cronies or one of his sleek young authors, she felt peevish and jealous.

Today, though, because Harry was eating with Evan Bright, Ann was more interested than jealous. Bright was a literary agent who brokered colossal deals for his writers that left them absurdly overpaid but usually sent their books quickly to the remainder bins in bookstores, where big orange 99¢ stickers were slapped over their titles. Evan Bright was a heavy man with circumflex eyebrows and a head of thick, swirly black hair, who liked to tell people how his cotton shirts were handmade for him by an ancient, opium-smoking Chinese tailor down on Pell Street. Bright had been a member of a lesser San Francisco psychedelic-rock band in the sixties. He had reportedly lived with Grace Slick for a while, then went off to Yale to study Renaissance Art, escaping the draft because of a supposedly extreme case of asthma, which hadn't reappeared since the Summer of Love. Now Evan Bright was married to a rather ordinary, pretty woman named Christina, who had given birth to twin boys. As soon as the babies were born, Christina was never seen again; she was remanded to their loft, nursing the twins like the She-Wolf of Rome, while Evan was off lobbing canapés into his mouth at book parties or enjoying bloated, three-hour lunches with Harry Corning.

Evan Bright was disgusting, everybody said so. He was a bad egg, and no one wanted to do business with him, but everyone did. He was evil incarnate, everyone said, but secretly, Ann liked him. He was always very friendly to her when he called to speak to Harry, and she felt free to joke around on the telephone with him, the way she would with her friends. Their conversations somehow made Ann feel noticed in a way that she otherwise never did at work. Ever since he had found out that she had gone to Yale, too, he would greet her with a heavily ironic "Boola, boola" when he called. "You know, I like you," Evan told her once. "You're smart. I'm keeping my eye on you, Rogoff."

Now Evan and Harry were hustling into Gepetto, already starting to remove their big-shouldered coats before they got through the door, while Ann and David watched from out on the street, like young Cathy and Heathcliff observing a fancy-dress ball through the window. They stood a moment, until the door silently sucked shut, and then they moved on.

That evening after work, David and Ann rode downtown, straphanging side by side, and when they got to her apartment they went straight to bed, as though out of duty to some notion of fledgling, hypersexed romance. She heard the familiar creak of the rolling ladder as they climbed up into her loft. Almost nobody Ann knew slept in a real bed; most people her age who lived in the city slept in a loft, or on a futon on the floor, or else on a fold-out couch. David had already taken off all his clothes and his eyeglasses, leaving them on a chair below the loft. When he appeared now, hoisting himself up onto the mattress, she felt as though the two of them were stowaways in the cargo hold of a steamer.

There was very little room to move up here in the loft. David flopped on top of her, kissing her neck and her mouth, and eventually he unrolled a condom from a box that featured a man and woman romping in a field of wheat. Ann, Meredith, and Lisa had recently paid a visit to a condom boutique in the Village called the Rubber Baron, where rum punch-scented condoms and simulated alligator leather condoms (with their Braille-like corrugation that promised "extra pleasure") were on display beside good old Trojans. A bored man with a shaved head sat behind the counter reading *Daniel Deronda*. How could you tell your parents that you worked in a condom store? How could you put the condom store on your résumé when applying for a new job? But the store was lively, and no one looked even remotely embarrassed to be there. Everyone stood pouring over bins of condoms like bargain-hunters at a white sale. This was the future for a generation of terrified consumers. They had no choice; unsheathed sex was a thing of the past. Ann had two friends from college who were HIV-positive; one was ailing, and the other was nervously healthy, pumping himself full of vitamins, eating a macrobiotic diet that required him to eat only those foods that grew in the soil near his home, which was Hoboken, New Jersey. Ann and Meredith and Lisa all felt occasional gusts of terror about AIDS, which they were usually able to dismiss. It seemed unlikely that any of them had been infected, although it wasn't impossible. There had been a TV movie about a girl who had gotten the disease from one encounter—*her first*—and they had all sat in front of the TV, watching in terror and sobbing. Now they all focused their attention on the future, and the future lay in condoms. Everyone had to bundle up these days, as if to brace for a long, long winter. So if you had to use something, why not make it rum punch?

Now David thrust forward into Ann, but the loft made sex very tricky. Each time he approached, his head smacked against the ceiling. "Shit!" he said the first time. "Shit!" he said the second time, and the third time it happened, he simply winced, mouthing the word. The entire episode was like this: somebody's head bumping against the ceiling, somebody in danger of falling out of bed. Passion didn't sweep them away, didn't carry the vessel with these two stowaways out into the middle of a glistening sea forever. Instead, they were so close to the ceiling that Ann could hear the twenty-month-old who lived upstairs padding around on the floor. "Bad dog," she heard the child say. *"Bery* bad."

"Does baby want to nursey?" the mother asked.

Nursey! This mother was probably going to breastfeed this child straight through adulthood, his legs dangling down as she held him on her lap, like the "Pièta." Why was Ann listening to this intimate domestic moment? She shouldn't be listening, she should be so deeply lost in her own private rapture with David that all other sounds were obliterated—desire like stoppers in her ears, a blindfold on her eyes, so that the only thing she could do was feel those sensations and cry out those things that people were supposed to cry out in the mindless middle of sex. She thought of Meredith in bed with Alan Seymour. She tried to imagine what Meredith was like in bed, and she made an effort to imitate her.

"Ohh," Ann said aloud, testing out the sound of it. "Ohhh." She released the syllable like an exhale.

"Ohh," David said in response. They were like two dogs howling to each other at night from separate back-yards.

In the apartment above, there was silence, then a rustle. "Baby" had obviously begun nursing. Then, suddenly, there was a thud of footsteps. The father. "Gail, did you bring home the Stovetop Stuffing?" his deep voice asked.

"Oh, I forgot," she answered.

"You know I like that stuffing." This was said with childlike petulance; he should have a suck on her other breast.

"All right already," Gail said. "It's not a felony, is it? Is it so terrible that I forgot? Where are you going? Michael? Michael?"

His footsteps moved away. Oh, the small tragedies of other people's lives, Ann thought as David slid down her body. He opened her legs and began lapping lightly at her, but this only made Ann feel as though she was being tickled. She tried to pretend she liked it, she tried to relax, but his feather-strokes were excruciating, and she felt laughter rising up inside her in a big whirlwind. Suddenly, out it came. "Hee hee hee hee hee," she laughed. She couldn't help herself, she couldn't stop, even when he picked up his head in bewilderment and just stared at her. "David, I'm sorry," she said. "I'm really sorry."

"Was it something I did?" he asked.

"No, no, it's not you, it's *me*," said Ann. "I'm just very ticklish, all of a sudden. I can't explain it."

"Well, that's a real esteem-builder," said David. "A real sexual confidence pick-me-up. Take a woman to bed and watch her hoot with laughter!"

He sat up in the loft and his head slammed into the ceiling. "Fuck!" he yelled, and upstairs the baby began to cry.

Weeks later, sitting in a movie theater with Meredith and Lisa, Ann said, "I think I take David for granted. He isn't boring, and he's totally considerate. Yesterday he volunteered to go to the dry cleaner's because they ruined my blouse and I was too scared to confront them myself. He even scrubbed out my humidifier, and it was growing spores."

"So what's the problem?" Meredith asked.

"Is it sexual?" Lisa asked, with some delicacy.

The lights dimmed, and they dutifully looked up at the movie screen, where a cartoon bucket of popcorn and a jumbo Coke were dancing. "Oh, maybe it is," said Ann. "It's like we're two good friends who happen to have sex. If the sex went away, I don't think either of us would notice."

"Well," said Lisa, "do you have . . . *you* know." She couldn't finish her question.

"She wants to know do you have orgasms," said Meredith. "I'm her simultaneous interpreter."

"Well, he does," said Ann. "And I'm . . . working on it." She looked at them pleadingly. "Did that ever happen to either of you?"

"Hardly," said Meredith. "I've been told I'm unusually responsive. It takes me like ten seconds. Which I suppose is a good thing, because that's how long Alan can ever stay. I'm practically still *thrashing,* and he's hailing a cab."

Ann turned to Lisa and asked, "What about with you and Eric?"

"I guess we're pretty well-matched," said Lisa, and then, inexplicably, she began to smirk. Meredith and Ann looked at her and Lisa said, "It's just, well, there was this nineteenth-century sex manual that Eric found in the library, and it had all these hilarious diagrams. . . ." At this point, Lisa collapsed into laughter and private, thrilled memory. A woman in the row ahead of them swiveled around and said, with full-bodied annoyance, "Do you *mind*?" Lisa apologized, and the woman swiveled back.

"Jesus, the movie hasn't even started yet," said Ann. "She needs to hear every word that comes out of a cartoon box of Good and Plenty?"

"Remember when we went to see *Love Story*?" asked Lisa. "Meredith was sobbing so loud that the whole theater started shushing her."

"Well, it was a very sad movie," Meredith said.

"What did Ali MacGraw have, leukemia?" asked Lisa. "Let me tell you, that is not what leukemia looks like. I've seen leukemia."

"I've seen leukemia and I've seen rain," sang Ann.

Lisa continued the line for her: "I've seen lymph nodes that I thought would never drain."

"You know," said Meredith, "I always thought that if I was given a chance, I could cure James Taylor's drug problem."

"Can you cure world hunger, too?" asked Ann.

"But of course you can't change men," said Meredith.

"Gosh, that's deep," said Ann.

"But you know I'm right," Meredith went on. "You really think things are going to change between you and David?"

"I don't know," Ann said, and she suddenly felt miserable.

"Nothing changes," said Meredith. "The married ones stay married, and you wind up with nothing. *Nada.* You turn into one of those bitter middle-aged women. Unwanted, dried up. At your sexual peak, but with no one to peak with. Getting your sexual kicks from a variety of small G.E. appliances."

The woman in front of them swiveled around a second time. "I'm not kidding!" she said. "You girls pipe down or I'll call someone."

"Well," said Ann, "that settles the question. We're still girls."

The movie began then, and everyone abruptly stopped speaking. But as they faced forward in the darkness, each had an image in her head: an overachieving male doctor pumping away at a rowing machine, a middle-aged married man pulling on his pants and going home, and a sweet-natured editorial assistant climbing into a loft for another night of temperate, boring love. When Meredith, Lisa, and Ann went home tonight, their men would be waiting.

Four

oth breakups were swift, but one was simple and the other was not. First came Meredith's; she and Alan were at the rink at Rockefeller Center, standing on the landing above the action, watching the skaters etch patterns below. It had been years since she herself had worn ice skates, but she could still remember knotting the laces so that the cuff of the boot cinched hard around her ankle, then wobbling out on that rubber flooring until she reached the gate of the rink, wearing a little skirt trimmed with blue rabbit fur. Now the idea of that skirt sickened her, brought to mind an image of underpaid factory workers in Taiwan dipping rabbit skins in vats of iridescent blue. Meredith regularly gave money to a has-been TV actress whose cause was animal rights, and who sent form letters and photographs of dogs shackled to laboratory slabs. But when Meredith was young, she had worn a blue rabbit fur skirt and matching blue rabbit fur pom-poms bobbing on her skates, and in all her rabbity glory she thought she was the most desirable being on ice. As she started her first lap around the rink, she waved to her parents, who quickly became a blur of heads and hats as Meredith began moving faster than they'd ever dreamed of going. Now she stood completely still in slate-gray Manolo Blahnik pumps beside Alan, who looked around furtively.

"Relax," she told him. "No one is going to recognize you."

"You never know," Alan said. "That woman's carrying a public TV tote bag."

"We could go skating," she suggested.

"I don't skate, Meredith," said Alan. "I have weak ankles."

"You can never do anything," Meredith said. "Even my best friend Lisa—whose boyfriend I wouldn't be caught dead with, he's such an anal-retentive jerk—at least she gets to go places with him. At least they have a life."

"I'm sorry," said Alan. "What do you want me to say?"

"Nothing. Nothing. Alan, I want to go home."

"Let me come with you," he said. "Hannah doesn't expect me until six."

"What happens at six?" she asked.

"We have to set up. We're having a little dinner party."

"A dinner party? Tonight?" Meredith drew away from him. "That means that right now your wife is walking around sticking toothpicks into little pieces of cheese."

"So?" he said.

"So, I want to stick toothpicks into little pieces of cheese!" said Meredith. "Is that so much to ask?"

"Meredith, please," said Alan. "People are looking at us. The woman with the *tote bag* is looking at us."

"So? Let them look," she said. "Even if someone sees us, they're not seeing anything. This is totally innocent."

"Oh?" he said.

"Yes," she answered. "Because starting right now, you and I are broken up."

A few weeks later, Ann and David disentangled themselves from each other very easily, then returned to separate sides of their divider at Eberhardt Publishers, where David still occasionally let paper clips rain down into Ann's hair. As far as he was concerned, they could have gone on and on as lovers forever. Sleeping at her apartment, clambering up into her loft, all of it was fine with him. His own apartment was a share with two other men, a railroad flat on Riverside Drive that had been broken into three times already. Now there were gates on all the windows, and no matter what time of day it was, there was a decent chance you would run into one of David's roommates walking around in just his underpants, eating a tangerine and idly pulling at his crotch, until he realized someone else was present.

Ann broke up with David on a late Sunday afternoon, on the D train crossing from Brooklyn into Manhattan. They had just been to a party given by Emily Rosten, a friend of David's from college. The occasion was the publication of a book of poetry by Emily's lover, an intense older woman named Candice Moore. There were copies of her book, *Womon to Womon,* propped up on the surfaces of furniture all around the apartment. On the back of the jacket, Candice Moore stared out furiously from her photograph as though posing for an ad for a women's self-defense academy. Emily came over and David introduced them, explaining that he and Emily had been friends since childhood. David used to visit her at

Swarthmore, and everyone assumed he was her boy-friend.

"You went to Swarthmore?" said Ann. "Did you know Ken Dowling?"

"Kind of short, laughed a lot?" asked Emily. "I think so."

"I've heard," said Candice, "that the Ken doll was actually named after a real person. But he didn't make any money off it, so he's very bitter. He lives in the Village. A friend of mine showed me his house."

"Yes, I think I've seen it," said Emily. "It's the one with the handle on the roof."

Ann liked this woman immediately. She was very funny and appealing, and Ann would have liked to talk to her more but Candice whisked Emily off to have her help set up chairs for an impromptu reading from *Womon to Womon*. A little while later, the guests gathered around good-naturedly to listen, while Candice began the first poem:

> *I am a river*
> *I come forth with great rushing water*
> *Do not be afraid to put your foot in*
> *I am a river*
> *I am a womon who lives in Brooklyn*
> *Here are the keys to my apartment.*

Later, after they'd managed to leave, Ann and David sat side by side on the clattering train. "That poetry went on forever," David said. "And I can't believe there's anyone left spelling 'woman' like that. Does she change everything? Manhattan would be *Mon*hattan. The wine would be *Mon*aschevitz."

"Maybe she's *mon*ic depressive," said Ann. She thought about Candice and Emily, the easy way they stood together. "They seem happy," she said. "I wonder what it would be like, being gay."

"I tried it once," said David. "In prep school. So now I can put the mandatory sensitive, homoerotic scene in my novel." He told her how a boy named Hodgins had developed a crush on him, slipping love letters in David's locker after soccer practice. One of the letters had read: *Dear David, I like the way you play soccer. And you smell nice. Hodge.* David explained how Hodge's letters kept piling up, and how one day he took the other boy up on the offer, accompanying him to a spot behind the field-house at dusk, when no one else was around, and spending half an hour groping and being groped in the scratchy grass, their school shirts hiked up, their pants opened, belts lolling.

" 'You smell nice'?" said Ann. "He said that?"

"Why, don't you think I smell nice?" asked David, and Ann realized that she'd never thought much about the way David smelled. "There are supposed to be these things, these pheromones, in men's armpits," David explained. "And when women inhale them, it turns them on."

"Meredith probably knows all about it," said Ann. "She can practically have an orgasm when a man opens a car door for her. Lisa too. She and Eric never leave the bed, except to perform surgery." She added, "I wish I was like that."

"You're fine," David said.

"I just think I'm missing something. I keep waiting for things to become thrilling."

"With me, you mean."

"Yes," said Ann slowly. "But I felt it before you, too."

"I think we're very relaxed together, sexually," said David.

"Cozy," said Ann. "Like Hansel and Gretel."

"Hansel and Gretel were brother and sister," David said.

"Well, sometimes I feel that way," Ann said. "It's all so familiar. So *nice.*"

"So what are you saying?" David asked. "You want to stop seeing me? You want us to be just friends?" She shrugged in apology. "Okay," he said after a moment. "I can live with that. So I guess I'll have to make a few changes in my novel. See, I had us getting married. A simple ceremony. We read selections from 'The Rubaiyat,' and then my cousin Naomi sings 'We've Only Just Begun.' She's pretty good. She was almost on 'Star Search.' "

"Meredith and Lisa have to be the bridesmaids," said Ann. "Of course, Meredith will be pissed that I'm getting married before her."

"Afterwards, there's lunch at a country club," said David. "Everyone gets a choice between fish or veal."

"My aunt Ilene will need a vegetable plate," warned Ann.

"Doesn't it sound great?" asked David. "And now I'll have to can the whole thing."

"I'm sorry," said Ann.

"I'll have to make you die a slow, painful death instead," said David. "Cyanide, maybe. A revenge plot. Yeah, that could work."

She poked him, and he poked her, and soon they were returning to the way they had once been. The train traveled slowly across the bridge, with Manhattan and all its possibilities spread out before them, now that they were free.

A month later, Meredith, Lisa, and Ann went home. *Home.* They still thought of it this way, even though none of them had lived in Magatuck for twelve years. Home was the place with central air conditioning and a reclining chair in the den. Home, in fact, was the place with a den. It was also the place where your parents still kept your ant farm on the windowsill of your childhood bedroom, the ants long dead and unmoving in a snaking, fossilized traffic jam.

The three of them met at Penn Station and boarded a train on the line they had taken their entire lives. They settled into a three-seater among all the weary commuters, men in stretchy gray suits reading the *Post,* and women in dress-for-success monkey suits and running shoes. As usual, Meredith took the window, Lisa sat in the middle, and Ann was left muttering about how she always wound up in the seat with no headrest. The train pulled out of the station and began its familiar, rocking trip from city to suburb. Shortly before they arrived in Magatuck, a man stood up, staring in their direction.

"Meredith, I think you have a new friend," whispered Lisa. "He's going to send you some crackling Szechuan beef." But the man was looking at all of them. He was middle-aged, with colorless hair. He looked extremely familiar. Could it be? They considered the possibility. It was, it was! Yes, it was Mr. Kern, who had taught hygiene at Magatuck High. Mr. Kern, who had lectured them all about gonorrhea, and showed them a short, memorable film about a teenaged girl named Amy who takes LSD and sets her hair on fire, while chanting in a childlike voice, "Look at the flames. Pretty, pretty flames . . ."

Mr. Kern had driven a black Corvette back then, and had told the class his first name (Neil), and one afternoon during a discussion of virginity, had haltingly admitted that he and his wife had had sex in college, before they were married. He was a young man who clipped articles from *Psychology Today* to read to his class, the kind of teacher to whom you could, in theory, go with a particularly humiliating problem, and he wouldn't shun you. He wore ties as wide as highways, and at the end of each class, sitting on his desktop, he quoted the "poetry" of Simon and Garfunkel aloud: " 'And a rock feels no pain/And an island never cries . . .' "

Now here he was, twelve years later, no longer young, no longer cool, weary because the new crops of students had gotten progressively meaner and stupider with each passing year. He smiled awkwardly at Meredith, Lisa, and Ann, and said an uncomfortable hello. "Well, what have you girls been up to lately?" he asked, and they each provided a stilted little verbal résumé. "Very nice, very nice," he said. "Weekdays, I'm still back in the high school. Same old same old." He thought for a moment. "I do an AIDS unit now," he added brightly. "That's new."

They all got off the train at Magatuck and waved goodbye in the parking lot. How sad to be Neil Kern, they thought as he unlocked the door of his little green two-door hatchback and drove off. What had happened to the Corvette? they wondered, imagining its fiberglass body lying twisted in a junkyard. They were just visitors to this franchise-filled hamlet, while he was stuck here forever. They felt smug and free as they watched his car leave the parking lot to join the early-evening river of traffic. For Meredith, Lisa, and Ann, this visit to Magatuck was just a lark; they had all been invited to Ann's parents' anniversary party, and tonight they would sleep in sleeping bags on the floor of Ann's childhood bedroom. This visit was quaint and painless and touching, and tomorrow they would visit Lisa's and Meredith's parents, before heading back to the city, where they belonged.

That night at the party, Ann's parents were toasted until one in the morning. The neighbors and friends and relatives who filled up the Rogoffs' living room cooed over Meredith, Lisa, and Ann, as though they were returning war heroes. "How's life in the Big Apple?" asked her uncle Sol.

"Fine," they answered in unison.

"Women in New York have to carry their purses like this," said Aunt Rita, and she crossed both arms over her chest as though clutching an imaginary pocketbook. An *ugly* imaginary pocketbook, Ann thought, yawning. She was exhausted, and so were her friends, but the older people kept on going. Her parents' friends were mostly retired and had begun keeping frathouse hours: up all night, slumbering until noon. Meredith, Lisa, and Ann could barely keep up with them. At one point, Ann's mother, Adele, came over and stood between Lisa and Meredith, her hands on both their shoulders. "Just look at you," she said. "Both of you, so sophisticated. One a brilliant doctor, the other one . . ." She paused, focusing on Meredith. "Beautiful," she finished. "Just beautiful."

"Thank you," Meredith said, lowering her eyes in pleasure. "You look terrific, too, Mrs. Rogoff."

Everyone had always told Ann what a sporty mother she had, and when she was younger this had made her proud, but now it mostly embarrassed her. Adele Rogoff was exactly five feet tall, played tennis three times a week, and her body was as hard and compact as a jockey's. She liked to linger at the various cosmetics counters at Bloomingdale's, pushing the little levers on those "computers" that supposedly could identify your skin type. Of all her daughter's friends, Meredith had always been her favorite, the one with true style. Whenever Adele saw Meredith, she looked at her for a long time, with an expression that might seem to an outsider to represent intense longing. She did crave Meredith, in some way, wishing that her own daughter might be transformed into such a stellar creature. If Adele had been Meredith's mother, what a wonderful time they would have! There would be marathon mother-daughter shopping days, the two women hoisting their oversized bags up into a booth as they nibbled at a communal Cobb salad in a department store restaurant. There would be heart-to-heart talks on the telephone late at night, and when Adele spoke about her troubles, her new, improved daughter would really listen.

The anniversary party was still going on when Ann, Meredith, and Lisa said good night and slipped upstairs to Ann's old bedroom, with its thick field of shag carpeting, its dust-catching white canopy bed, its ancient curling posters on the walls. The voices of Ann's relatives still burbled up from downstairs. There was nothing safer than going to sleep knowing that your parents were nearby having a good time with their friends. They should sell that tape to insomniacs, Ann thought: "Your Parents'

Party." "Relive the thrills, the chills, the laughter, the clanging of glasses, the 'adult' conversation." Meredith sat on Ann's bed, peering into a magnifying mirror, doing a quick critical study of her own face. "This pore is as big as the Sea of Tranquility," she muttered.

"God, would you put that mirror away?" asked Ann. Meredith put it down and they climbed into their sleeping bags, which were still cold, for they had been rolled up in the Rogoffs' garage since high school. The light was extinguished. "You know what's wrong with adulthood?" Ann said. "Not enough sleepovers. Remember that night when we wrote a song about Shelly Berkowitz?"

"Who?" asked Meredith.

"Shelly Berkowitz," said Ann. "I can't believe you don't remember. We were in orchestra together, and she wouldn't let anybody try her flute. She pretended to feel bad about it. She said that if it were up to her, she'd love to let us try it, but it was her father's rule, because the flute was really, really expensive. Then we ran into Mr. Berkowitz at the mall and asked him why he wouldn't let other kids try her flute, and he didn't know what we were talking about. It turned out that Shelly was just afraid of other people's saliva." Ann began to sing, to the tune of "Baby, You Can Drive My Car." "Shelly, let me play your flute/If you don't I'll have to shoot . . ."

Lisa joined in. "Shelly, let me play your flute/I won't give you cooties . . ."

Together they sang, "Toot toot and toot toot, yeah!"

Later, when they had stopped singing and laughing, and were lying on their backs in a circle, like the June Taylor Dancers in sleeping bags, Meredith said, into the darkness, "Right now, Alan is probably in bed with that woman."

"You mean his wife?" asked Ann. "Yeah, the nerve."

"Right now," said Lisa, "Eric's probably removing someone's spleen."

"I hate to sleep alone," Meredith said. "It doesn't feel natural. I think I truly, biologically, need to have a man in my life."

"A woman without a man is like a fish without a bicycle," said Ann.

"Now, that is the dumbest phrase of all time," Meredith said. "If we really didn't need men, then we would never shave under our arms, right? And we wouldn't go on diets. We'd just sit around wearing baggy clothes, eating Mallomars, and masturbating all day."

Ann said, thoughtfully, "That pretty much sums up my life."

"Oh, it does not," said Lisa. "You have a good life. You both do."

"This is not the life I wanted," said Meredith.

"Do you realize that if we suddenly ran into Barbara, she wouldn't have any idea of what our lives have been like all these years?" Lisa asked. "We'd have to tell her everything."

"What's to know?" Ann asked. "Not much has happened to me since I saw her last. Oh wait, that's not true. I got breasts. I could tell her that."

"I could tell her how I got fucked over by a fifty-four-year-old egotist," said Meredith.

"I could tell her," said Lisa, "that I'm getting married."

There was a sudden, shocked silence.

"Yeah," she continued. "Eric and I are engaged. We want to make it official. We're both going to be gerontologists and have a joint practice. We really think alike. We care about the same things."

"Oh my God," was all Ann could manage to say.

"It was bound to happen sooner or later," Meredith said. "The beginning of the end."

" 'The beginning of the end'? I'm not going to a *gulag*," said Lisa. "I'm just getting married."

"Just?" said Meredith. "Don't you know what marriage is, Lisa?"

"Apparently you do, Meredith," Ann said. "Ever since you got that degree in marriage counseling from Heidelberg."

"Marriage," said Meredith, "is a curtain that drops down between you and your friends. It separates you from them forever."

"Well, congratulations," said Ann.

"Thank you," said Lisa.

"I mean, I'm happy for you and everything," said Ann, "but you'll have to forgive me. This just seems so impetuous. So madcap. It's not like you."

"Do I always have to be the boring one?" asked Lisa.

"You're not the boring one," said Ann.

"Then what am I?"

"You're the nice one," Meredith said.

"And I'm the smart one," said Ann. "And Meredith is the beautiful one. Put us all together, and we're Miss Universe."

"I'm marrying Eric because I love him," said Lisa. "But can't I have him and you, too? Does it have to be like *Sophie's Choice*?"

"When the curtain falls," said Meredith, her voice lowered to a deep, dramatic hush, like a children's librarian during story hour, "it won't make a sound, but next thing you know, you're shrouded in darkness, away from the world of your friends. Gone are the days of girlhood.

Gone are the days of long telephone calls. Gone are the days of—"

"I'm not going to change!" cried Lisa. "Don't you believe me? I'm still a part of . . . this. Of us. Of Mer-LisAn." She began to sing, her voice a tender warble. "Oh, we're friends from the soul and we're friends from the heart . . ."

"This is not fair," said Ann. "I'm going to cry."

"We're friends forever and we're never gonna part," Lisa went on, and her voice grew louder now. "Mer-*hmm*LisAn/Mer*hmm*LisAn/Friends forever, Mer*hmm*-LisAn . . ."

They looked over at Lisa, who was wearing a long, wrinkled T-shirt. In the dim light of the room she looked so unadorned, so familiar. They each remembered the way, when she was twelve years old, she would take out her bite plate before bed—that lightweight twist of metal attached to an eerie cast of the roof of her mouth. She used to lay it on a tissue beside her sleeping bag. Her teeth were straight now, and in several months her mouth would open at night to kiss the mouth of the man she would call her husband.

The next day, as soon as she returned home, Meredith dialed Ann's number.

"Hello?" said Ann.

"So, can you believe it?" asked Meredith.

"Who is this?" Ann asked.

"Who is this? It's Meredith."

"Meredith? Meredith Guzzi?"

"What other Merediths do you know?"

"You never call me," said Ann.

"Well, this is an emergency," Meredith said. "We should have said something when we met him at Lisa's dinner party. Right then and there in her kitchen. And if that didn't work, we should have dragged her to a motel room and had her deprogrammed, like parents do when their kids become Moonies."

"We did say something," said Ann. "We told her he was 'moving.' So now she thinks she's marrying Schweitzer. We encouraged her, Meredith. We lied to her."

"Oh, God," Meredith moaned, "she's going to marry him, and probably have children with him—a whole litter of nerdy, anal-retentive children."

"What kind of friends are we?" asked Ann. "Friends from the heart? From the soul? Lisa is our best friend in the world, and she is making this terrible mistake, and now it's much too late to do anything. So you know what? We are fucked, Meredith."

Five

Wedding whites were very different from hospital whites. There was no beeper clipped to the white silk sash that bound Lisa's narrow waist, and no ID card attached to the bosom of her elaborate dress. She looked entirely happy, as though she was marrying someone appropriate for her, someone wonderful whom everyone could love. If you didn't know what Eric's personality was like, you might have felt that Lisa had landed the perfect groom: a handsome, soulful individual with long, doctorly fingers that were apparently capable of thrilling the bride. At the moment that Eric and Lisa moved together for their triumphant kiss, Meredith and Ann, dressed in purple bridesmaids dresses and standing to the side, both burst into tears.

Later, during the reception, the wedding photographer took an inordinate number of photos of Meredith, until Lisa's father pulled him aside and instructed him to turn his lens in the direction of the bride. Eric introduced everyone to his uncle Mort and his uncle Joel, who moved a bit closer to get a better look at Meredith's extraordinary complexion. "I can tell you're not one of the foolish ones," Uncle Joel said to her. "You use sun block, don't you?"

And Uncle Mort said, "Girls, we have a little saying in our family: 'If you have a wart, call Uncle Mort. If you have a mole, call Uncle Joel.' " Meredith had drunk a few glasses of champagne, and she laughed at this dumb little rhyme, then suddenly, inexplicably, wanted to weep.

Toward the end of the day, the band gamely played while a few couples still slow-danced, and waiters offered seconds of wedding cake to any takers. Meredith and Ann leaned against a column in the large, rented room. "You know," said Ann, "I kept waiting for that moment when they ask if anybody knows a reason why this couple should not be married. But they never really say that, do they?"

"Only in movies," said Meredith.

"I had it all planned," Ann said. "I would have shouted out, 'That man is too nerdy to marry our friend!' "

"You would not," said Meredith. "You would have just stood there, like we both did. Like idiots in these bridesmaids dresses. God, why did she pick purple?"

"She said it's Eric's favorite color," said Ann.

"Probably because it's the color of capillaries," said Meredith.

But she could see that Ann was no longer listening. Instead, she was gazing across the room, and Meredith followed her gaze to the place on the dance floor where Lisa and Eric were slow-dancing to the Beatles' song "In My Life." It almost felt invasive to watch this radiant couple floating gently around the floor, their love so clearly on exhibit. They were modest but still transparent in their feelings for each other, and neither Meredith nor Ann could turn away. If Eric and Lisa had been ice skaters, they would have left a spiral of circles in the ice with their skates, proof that love had made them move in such repetitive and dizzying ways.

Part Two

Six

*O*ne year later, Ann Rogoff took up lesbianism the way other people take an adult education course. It was like learning Indonesian cooking late in life, or calligraphy. At twenty-nine she became an expert on the subject, a willing participant in this new and unusual field. It happened so suddenly that she barely understood it; for so many years she was a heterosexual, keeping her eyes open to the possibilities of a man strolling into her life, and now, with very little effort on her part, she was a lesbian, looking at women on the street and thinking: *hmm.*

There was no way she could have become a lesbian quietly; quiet lesbianism was not a possibility for someone like Ann. She had to do it noisily, kicking and screaming, in a way that would frighten her mother and certainly gain the instant attention of both Meredith and Lisa. She knew she would not be able to explain her transformation to them, but she still had to try.

She had met Emily Rosten at the publication party for David's novel, *The Lean Years,* which Eberhardt had just published. David had quit his job the day he sold his novel. Harry Corning became his editor, and Evan Bright his agent, so Ann still had a lot to do with David, and they still remained good friends. His book was receiving serious, encouraging attention and had been excerpted in *The Paris Review.* In articles David came across as particularly vulnerable and sweet, like a brooding college student with death on his mind. She was glad he had become a success, but she still felt depressed at being the one who had to stay behind.

The publication party was held at a fussy-looking bookstore with oak paneling and moss-green carpet and a superior music system that piped in medieval church favorites. You could live in this bookstore; you could lie down in its dense carpet and read all night. At the party, the music was turned off for a moment and the guests became quiet, so that Harry Corning could make a toast to David. "For years," Harry began, "David Marcus made coffee, typed letters, and even knew how to change the paper in the copy machine. But I never knew he could write like a fucking angel."

After the toast, Ann congratulated David, then stepped toward a shelf of books, still holding her lightweight cup of bad wine in her hand, wondering if she could simply deposit it on a nearby surface in the Science section, when she noticed a woman absorbed in a book. The title was *The Sexual Life of Marine Animals,* and Ann smirked. The woman looked up, embarrassed. She was very pretty, with dark hair and a long, Mannerist neck, like Audrey Hepburn. "I saw the title and I couldn't resist," the woman said.

"So how is it?" Ann asked politely.

"Actually, very interesting. It says here that dolphins are promiscuous."

"You mean Flipper put out?" Ann asked.

"Oh yeah. But blue-green algae is extremely faithful," the woman said, closing the book. "It only has sex with itself."

"That's convenient," Ann found herself saying. "No need to send flowers the next day."

"I like sending flowers," said the woman.

What was this conversation about? What were they doing? Was this called flirting? It felt strange, as though they were flirting with each other according to the customs of another planet. Ann felt confused, almost drugged. "Well!" she said, her voice too loud, "I think I'll get me some more of those little cracker things." She turned away and headed toward the table where the tray of food lay, but the woman followed her there.

"Wait, I know you," the woman said. "You came to my house in Brooklyn. You were David's girlfriend."

"Oh, that was over a year ago," said Ann, and she nervously manipulated a canapé into the general direction of her mouth.

"Uh, you have a caper on your face," the woman said.

"Oh, God," said Ann. She took a swipe at herself and missed the spot.

"Lower," said the woman, whose name, Ann now recalled, was Emily. Ann tried again and missed.

"Here," said Emily, laughing, and she delicately picked Ann's hand up and guided it to the right spot.

"If my mother were here," said Ann, "she would remove it with some spit on a napkin. She's very Nanook of the North."

"You know, I remember you very well," said Emily.

"Why, did I have a caper on my face that day?"

"No, you were funny," said Emily. "You still are. Candice was pissed that I was talking to you. She was extremely possessive. Actually, I'm being nice. Candice was insane."

"Candice," said Ann. "Oh, the poet, right? That stuff about women being like lakes."

"Rivers," said Emily. "A crucial distinction."

"So," said Ann, "do you still live in Brooklyn?"

"No," said Emily. "Not anymore."

Later, in the dark, lively cave of a bar called Girls' Town, Ann and Emily Rosten stood at the bar drinking beers. Ann had been to gay bars before, but only men's bars, crowded with packs of untouchable men in button-fly jeans. Her gay male friends had encouraged Ann to accompany them to these bars, because they had only recently come out and felt frightened of going in alone. So she had chaperoned them, curious about the subculture and fond of the music, and within half an hour, her friends had invariably met other men, mumbling apologies to Ann as they left and offering to pay her cab fare home.

"If I was into boys," said Emily, "David is definitely the one I'd pick."

"Were you ever involved with boys? I mean men," asked Ann.

"Sure," said Emily. "But they tended to have long hair and be effeminate. Finally I figured it out. Why did you and David break up?"

"You know," said Ann vaguely. "A chemistry thing."

"What, he was missing molecules?" said Emily. "I think love is very simple. You're either attracted to someone or you're not. You can't fake it." Emily paused, looking across the room. After a moment, she said, "By the way, that woman is staring at you."

Ann looked. Across the room, a dark-haired woman was unabashedly watching Ann. "What do you think she wants?" Ann asked Emily in a whisper.

"Maybe she likes you," said Emily with a small, taunting smile.

"But I'm not . . . *you* know," said Ann.

"*That* way?" said Emily.

But it was too late to take this any further, because the woman stood and walked across the room and came right up to Ann. "Hi," she said.

"Hi," Ann said, meekly.

"Ann? Ann Rogoff? Don't you remember me?" the woman asked.

"I don't think so," answered Ann.

"This is a blast from your past," the woman said. "I'm Shelly. Shelly Berkowitz."

"Oh my God!" said Ann. "Shelly Berkowitz. You're the one who wouldn't let anybody try your flute."

"It wasn't my rule," Shelly said flatly, "it was my father's."

"We grew up together," Ann explained to Emily. "We were in orchestra."

"And now we meet again," said Shelly. "There must have been something in the water in Magatuck."

"Oh," said Ann, "but I'm not—" But just then another woman called to Shelly from across the room, and Shelly interrupted Ann, saying that she was glad to have seen her, and hoped she was doing well, but that she had to run. And with that, she turned and walked away, while Ann sat stunned from this encounter. "Shelly Berkowitz," she kept repeating. "I just can't get over it. Oh great, now she thinks I'm gay. She'll probably tell her mother where she saw me, and then my mother will read about it in the Magatuck newspaper: 'Local girl nabbed in raid on lesbian bar.' "

Emily laughed, and added, "Although the suspect claimed she's not 'that way,' she appeared to be having a suspiciously good time."

Sex with a woman wasn't all that different from sex with a man. The only real difference was, it was better. Much better. By the aquamarine light of the digital clock beside Emily Rosten's bed, Ann discovered this fact for herself. They had been up half the night, engaging in odd thrashing activities that resulted in surprisingly familiar thrills, as though she had done this before, in an earlier life. *Maybe I was Gertrude Stein,* she thought giddily. *Maybe I was Eleanor Roosevelt.* (Ann had always enjoyed the play *Sunrise at Campobello.*) In addition to the sex being so exciting, it was also safe. Supposedly. True, there was a product on the market now called a dental dam, which was basically a pup tent that needed to be pitched inside the vagina, but using one seemed a little extreme. Maybe she was kidding herself, but sex between women seemed far removed from AIDS anxiety. It seemed far removed from the whole world, Ann thought.

If Adele Rogoff had seen her daughter making love to another woman, she would have let loose a series of hideous, woman-warrior screams, then whirled in a circle until she turned into a puddle of butter like the tigers in

"Little Black Sambo," then disappeared completely. But Adele Rogoff was safely sleeping with her husband back in Magatuck, their bodies lying in relaxed, slovenly, sack-of-flour positions, much the way that Ann's and Emily's were right now. Without moving her head, but instead peering sideways, Ann checked to see if Emily was awake. No. Emily was fast asleep, the pillow crushed against her face, the slope of one shoulder poking up over the quilt. The entire room hissed and clanked with the efforts of steam in the radiator. Ann replayed the evening, starting with the meeting at David's party, progressing through the drink in the bar, and the startling and wonderful kiss on the front stoop of a brownstone, and winding up back here, in the bedroom of Emily's apartment. Ann felt that there ought to be some ritual to commemorate her first lesbian experience. In the old days, people hung bloodied bedsheets out the window after their first night of married love. Maybe lesbians could hang *clean* bedsheets out their window. Somehow, Ann finally fell asleep, dreaming of bedsheets, and bare-breasted women, and her mother's looming face, the mouth open wide in pure, suburban horror.

In the morning, Ann woke up to the buzz of an electric razor. "Oh," said Emily, coming awake, "that's Lloyd. Or maybe Steven."

"Who?" said Ann.

"My roommate and his boyfriend," said Emily. "Didn't I tell you?"

Lloyd Vendler was studying to be a psychoanalyst. All day he sat in his tiny bedroom in the apartment, taking a yellow Hi-Liter pen to the writings of Freud. He was a tall man with reassuring good looks, and his boyfriend, Steven Karp, was a short, slight, worried character actor, who had appeared on a few commercials, always playing a harried young dad. But lately, work was scarce, and Steven supported himself by working as a roller-skating waiter at an Upper West Side restaurant.

After Emily introduced Ann all around, the foursome sat down to breakfast together. Ann knew she was being watched, interviewed, especially by Steven. She didn't mind, though, because she still felt so excited, that everything else was merely background noise. Emily cooked a big pot of McCann's Irish oatmeal, which Ann happily ate, even though breakfast usually sickened her. She felt as though she were back in college, sitting around a sticky table in the dining hall before class slowly eating a Pop Tart and smoking a cigarette. She realized how much she missed that feeling; after college, you were truly on your own. Inseparable clusters of friends broke up and scattered. You wolfed down breakfast by yourself, or not at all. But now Ann imagined herself becoming ensconced in this household, sitting here each morning in Emily's corduroy bathrobe, uttering barbed comments and eating Irish oatmeal. *Count me in,* she thought. *Sign me up.*

Over breakfast, Steven practiced for an audition. "It's for waffles," he explained to Ann. "See, I'm this father at breakfast, and I've got three kids. It's my wife's birthday. We're letting her sleep. At any rate, we're *supposed* to let her sleep." He paused, putting his hands up to his face as though to clear his features and let the persona of Generic TV Dad take over. " 'Okay, kids,' " he began. " 'Who wants waffles? Whaddya mean, my waffles are boring? Whaddya mean, *Mom's* waffles are better? These are Butterfield's waffles. So good that not even a dad can ruin 'em.' " When he was done, he looked around the table.

"So?" he asked. There was silence. "Nu? What do you think?"

"I think," said Emily, "that that is an unconscionably sexist commercial."

"Sexist! Why? It's the man who's the schmuck," said Steven. "The woman is in charge. The sleeping mother. The dormant goddess. She's the one they all worship."

"Why should the onus of good waffle-making be on the woman?" said Emily. "I can't believe you're going to that audition."

"Well," said Lloyd, "it pays well, and Steven needs to make money. You know about that production of *Mourning Becomes Electra* that's coming up. He's got to support himself between real plays."

"Mourning Becomes Electra," said Emily, "is extremely hostile to women. O'Neill had a real problem with women. His mother was insane. And besides, it's going to be performed in someone's *loft.* This isn't exactly the Actor's Studio we're talking about."

"You are so critical," said Steven. "You're the only one who can do no wrong." He turned to Ann. "This is what breakfasts are like around here," he said. "You can still turn back, you know. There's still time to make your escape from the International House o' Homos."

"I don't want to leave," Ann said.

"You don't?" said Emily. "That's great."

Ann lingered at the apartment for half the day, lying in Emily's bed, listening to ancient folk-rock record albums from their separate but similar girlhoods, until finally there came a point at which Ann wanted to be alone. She wanted to go home and take a shower, and look over a manuscript she had brought home from work this weekend. But mostly she wanted to be alone so she could figure out how in the world she was going to explain everything to Meredith and Lisa.

At the Lucky Wok, two nights later, Ann broke the news. She had been unable to imagine a subtle segue that would make the moment smooth and free of awkwardness. She decided, finally, that she was making much too much of the whole matter. Her friends were adults. They knew about lesbians, and besides, love was love, Ann told herself. *Love was love,* she said, reciting the words like a mantra, but she knew this was moronic. Love was love; so what? Death was death, too, but that didn't make it any easier to understand. Emily had said that if Ann was so nervous about telling her friends, then maybe she shouldn't tell them. Maybe it should remain a secret for now. But Ann knew that any experience that hadn't been tested out on Meredith and Lisa wasn't really an experience at all. It was like that tree falling in the forest, and possibly not making a sound. If Lisa and Meredith weren't around to hear Ann's news, then maybe it wasn't news at all. Maybe Emily didn't even exist; maybe Ann had been to bed with a hologram.

Ann needed to tell them, and she needed to tell them right away, so she simply jumped in without a preamble. They were fussing over what to order at the Lucky Wok, but Ann couldn't think about food. "We could split an order of Happy Family," Lisa was saying.

"Why do they call it that?" asked Meredith. "Nobody comes from a Happy Family. They should call it Five Miserable People in a Station Wagon."

Suddenly Ann spoke. "I have an announcement," she said.

Lisa and Meredith continued reading their menus. "What is it?" Lisa asked, not looking up.

"I don't know how to say it," said Ann. "It's all so strange. But I just have to talk about it or I'll explode."

Meredith and Lisa lowered their menus. "Does this involve a UFO sighting?" Meredith asked.

"I'm having an affair with a woman," said Ann. "I think I'm a lesbian." Meredith and Lisa kept looking at her, unblinking. "Well, aren't you going to say something?" asked Ann.

"You are not a lesbian," said Meredith.

"Excuse me?"

"I mean, I'm glad you finally ended your celibacy marathon," said Meredith, "but you can't just wake up one morning and decide you're a lesbian."

"You're right," said Ann. "I have to earn a few merit badges first."

"First of all," said Meredith, "there would have been signs."

"What," said Lisa, "an old gypsy woman would have appeared at a fork in the road?"

"And I would have been very attracted to her," said Ann.

"You know," said Lisa nervously, "I read in a journal that scientists have discovered this entire flock of lesbian seagulls."

"In case you don't remember, Meredith," said Ann, "I was sexually unfulfilled with David. And besides, I had crushes when I was little."

"I think it was off the coast of Maine," Lisa went on.

"The birds were necking on a sandbar."

"Crushes?" said Meredith, all suspicious. "On who?"

"On Julie Andrews," said Ann. "She looked very beautiful in *The Sound of Music*. I told my mother I wanted to be a nun, too, but she said they'd never take me because I was a Jewish girl, and that's all I'd ever be. But I always imagined living on that mountain with Julie Andrews. We'd be nuns together. It would be very peaceful."

"You had a crush on *Julie Andrews*?" said Lisa. "That seems illegal."

Suddenly, two waiters wheeled over a cart that had flames shooting up from it. They stopped in front of Meredith. "Lady," said one of the waiters, "the gentleman over there asked us to send you this. Crispy flaming duck."

"Oh, that's very sweet," said Meredith, "but I really can't accept it. You'll have to take it back."

"He says he likes your TV show," the waiter persisted.

"Oh?" said Meredith. "Which gentleman?"

Ann slammed her chopsticks down on the table and said, "I do not fucking believe this!" The waiters quickly rolled the cart away, the sizzling softening to a quiet hiss, the flames dying down. "We were talking about *my* life," Ann continued, "and once again the focus has completely shifted to Meredith, the star of public TV!"

"I'm not a star," said Meredith. "It's a local show. And can I help it? Did I ask for crispy flaming duck?"

"No," said Ann, "but I'm sure you didn't mind the interruption, because you can't stand to listen to me when I talk. I have had an experience that has opened me up sexually, and politically, and neither of you has even asked me her goddamn name!" She was in tears now.

"We're sorry, Ann," said Lisa. "Please tell us her name."

"No," said Ann. "You missed your chance."

"All right, I'll start with the *A*'s," said Lisa. "Abby . . . Adele . . . Anita . . ."

"Amazon," offered Meredith.

"Her name is Emily, all right?" said Ann. "She's a lawyer and she looks like Audrey Hepburn. She's very politically active, and we're going to a protest against homophobia at City Hall. It's a kiss-in."

"A kiss-in?" asked Lisa. "Everybody kisses each other? In public?" Ann nodded.

"Tongues?" said Meredith, aghast.

"You are so immature, Meredith," said Ann.

"Oh, come off it," Meredith said. "How can we take you seriously? You've always gone through these phases. It's just like the time you became a Buddhist, and you insisted that we call you Savita."

"Sativa," said Ann.

"It lasted three days," said Meredith, "and you'd already bought a lifetime supply of incense."

"Ann," Lisa tried, "I think what Meredith is trying to say is—"

"Believe it or not," Meredith interrupted, "I look at women on the street, too. Everybody does. But it doesn't mean I want to go to bed with them. It usually means I want to know where they bought their clothes. Call me old-fashioned, but I guess I'm content just being heterosexual."

"You, content?" said Ann. "Meredith, all you do is complain. Remember that guy who made you go to the Renaissance Fair? And he brought along a bottle of wine and insisted on calling it 'mead'? Or that other guy, who sent you that pornographic fax at work and everybody saw it?"

"So," said Meredith, "I have a few problems with men. But obviously you do, too."

"Not anymore," said Ann.

Seven

*Y*ou think you know somebody, and then *bam,*" said Lisa. "They drop the bomb, and everything changes."

"Do you realize," said Meredith, "that all those nights when we had sleepovers, and we got undressed in front of each other, she was probably gay the entire time. And she saw my breasts, Lisa, my breasts!" She paused. "Oh my God!" she added, as if in afterthought.

"Okay, so she saw your breasts," said Lisa. "Relax. It's not like she's going to jump you."

"No, not that," said Meredith. "This!" She pointed up, toward the row of advertisements on the subway wall. There, between an ad for hemorrhoid cream and one for Goya beans, was a picture of Lisa's husband, Eric. Beneath Eric's picture were the words IF YOU HAVE BAD SKIN, CALL DR. ZINN, followed by the phone number 238-SEBA.

"Oh yeah," mumbled Lisa. "I didn't see that one."

"Why didn't you tell us Eric was running ads?"

"I guess I thought you'd say it was tacky," Lisa said.

"But you know, it's really hard starting a practice in New York. Dermatology is very competitive."

Eric had begun running these ads a month earlier, and to Lisa's relief, neither Meredith nor Ann had stumbled upon them until now. Meredith, of course, rarely rode the subway anymore, since she'd become a minor TV personality, and Ann probably had her head in a book whenever she was on a train. But now Eric had been found out, and Lisa felt an odd mix of shame and defensiveness, as though her husband had been revealed to be a Nazi collaborator, instead of merely a dermatologist looking for a few new faces. Meredith and Lisa both sat and stared silently up at Eric's face, and Lisa was reminded of the night that he had decided to quit gerontology. He had come home from work at eleven, hungry and cranky and ranting about old people, how annoying they were with their constant questions, their loose grip on lucidity, their emphatically human smells, the way their worried, grown children would pull you aside and belligerently demand to know everything you were doing for their parents, step by step. Eric had always complained about these things, and had even had a recurring dream in which Jessica Tandy and Hume Cronyn are chasing him with a net, but his aggravation had become a sort of white noise within their marriage, which she assumed would always be there.

Old people loved Lisa; after they remarked on how young she looked, with her unlined face and headband, they actually listened to her, and obeyed her requests that they take their medication, or give up salt. She was so familiar to them that they wanted to please her. She spent a few extra moments listening to them talk about their children, or how much it used to cost to ride the subway when they were her age, and sometimes she even listened as they talked feverishly about how the coloreds had ruined the city. She had once played a lengthy, excruciating game of canasta with a woman whose eyes were milky-blind from cataracts. Lisa was attentive and returned calls quickly. Her handwriting on her prescription pad was legible, even loopily girlish, and she threw herself into this difficult work inside the big clanking machine of this scary urban hospital, knowing that someday she would be old too, and would probably be spat on by some arrogant young doctor who was squeamish about old people and the way they smelled.

If Eric felt anything similar, he didn't let on. He just wanted out. So he switched to dermatology, and the change in him was miraculous. He slept better at night, and he pulled at the oars of his rowing machine with new vigor. But he had disappointed her, and he knew it. She even wondered if she would be able to keep loving him. Now she looked at his face on the wall, trying to connect it with the man she loved. This face would be there tonight when she came home, and yet when she saw it under the harsh fluorescence of the train, she felt only a vague, mortifying desire to slide a few discreet feet away from his picture, to pretend she didn't know this man. His hairline was receding, and she realized she was getting tired of his beard. She had never seen one-third of his face—he, who dealt exclusively in skin.

He looked like a decent person, she thought, staring at the picture, although maybe not as nice as the woman on the ad beside his, the Hispanic housewife who held up a can of Goya beans and gazed dreamily at it, as though at a lover. Eric looked nice, and sanitary, and responsible, and she knew that no matter what, he would remain a good doctor. He had nimble hands and was thorough in his exams. But she kept thinking how the picture on the wall looked like someone's graduation photo from Accounting and Payroll School. To a straphanger riding sleepily home from work, eyes sweeping across the wall of ads, Eric's face might appear boring. The straphanger might keep looking right past Eric, settling instead on the happy lady from Goya.

Was Eric boring? Lisa felt so tender toward him and all his anxieties and obsessions. When they lay in bed at night and held each other, she enjoyed being young and married and naked, their bodies as cool as pillows when you first lay down your head. They talked in shorthand about medicine, and they commiserated about malpractice insurance, and they made love and sometimes, afterward, they began their nighttime theater, which involved a cast of characters they had invented when they first became lovers, and which had expanded and deepened over the years, like the characters on a long-running soap opera. Lisa wondered if every couple had such games, but she couldn't dare ask anyone; it was too personal, and even worse, somehow, than sharing details of their sex life.

The game had begun with a name for Lisa's diaphragm. "Princess Di," Eric had dubbed it once, when she came back from the bathroom with the thing in. That name launched a dialogue between "Princess Di" and the "Royal Sceptre," which was, of course, a name for Eric's penis. From there, it wasn't long before they had added other characters based on various body parts and household objects, until they had created an idiotic universe unknown to anyone else. There was the Loofah Man, Mrs. Butterworth, and several others, each one speaking in a distinct voice. This was a side of Eric that

Meredith and Ann would never see, which was probably just as well.

Meredith and Lisa sat in silence for a while, and finally Meredith said, "Nothing's come out the way it was supposed to. Eric's a dermatologist. Ann's a dyke. You know, Lisa, things are going to be different now between Ann and us. Even socially."

"How so?" Lisa asked.

"Well, take our dinners at the Lucky Wok," said Meredith. "Eric never comes, because it's a girls' night out, right? But Emily *is* a girl, sort of. So maybe she's going to want to come, too. And the whole dynamic will change. We'll have to try to include her in the conversation."

"I hear she speaks a little English, Meredith," Lisa said.

"And suppose I give a dinner party with a lot of influential people from the station," said Meredith. "Am I supposed to invite Ann and Emily? We usually sit boy-girl. This would screw up the seating plan. And wouldn't it look strange, introducing them as a couple?" She closed her eyes, as though trying to imagine the moment. "No, wait," she suddenly said, "maybe it would look exotic, like I have a fascinating bunch of friends. A salon, like Paris in the twenties!"

"I didn't know you give dinner parties," Lisa said. "You never invite me."

"Yes I do," said Meredith uneasily.

"What, that pot-luck thing, where five different people brought falafel?" said Lisa. "That was years ago."

They sat in protracted, embarrassed silence, Eric looming above them. Finally Meredith said, "Why did he pick 238-SEBA? Does it stand for something?"

"Sebaceous glands," said Lisa. "They make your skin break out."

"Why not 238-ZITS?" asked Meredith.

Lisa sighed. Then she said, "ZITS was taken."

It wasn't hard to like Ann's lover, or to even understand why Ann liked her. Emily was almost as good-looking as Meredith, Lisa realized with some satisfaction. When Meredith and Lisa first met Emily, they had both been shocked, imagining some shrill, taut, angry woman with a freshly shaved head, and finding instead this beautiful, articulate woman with terrific clothes. Meredith had told Lisa that the fact of Emily depressed her a little, and this gave a secret power to Ann, placing her above Meredith on the food chain of sophistication.

Ann and Emily had quickly become a lesbian poster couple, attending Queer Nation kiss-ins and sit-ins and die-ins, lying down among dozens of others at the entrance to the Holland Tunnel, stopping the flow of rush-hour traffic and appearing on the six o'clock news. Winnie Jarret, the insipid reporter on the local news show, had thrust a microphone right up in front of the couple, and Ann had spoken easily into it, as though she had been an activist for years, as though she had grown up in a house where secret radical meetings were held in the basement, and Paul Robeson sometimes stopped by for a home-cooked meal. "We're here today," Ann said into Winnie's mike, "because this is something we believe in. We and our gay brothers and lesbian sisters have been oppressed far too long." Ann had learned her oratorical style not from a history of activism but from her valedictory speech at Magatuck High School, when she had stood up and read the essay she had written for the occasion, called "We Hold These Truths."

Ann brought Emily everywhere, even to their next dinner at the Lucky Wok. Everyone was cheerful and polite and restrained throughout the meal, but the delicate pH balance had suddenly changed, and Lisa hoped that Emily would not come to dinner the following month. This wasn't fair, Lisa knew; of course they had to open their world to include other people. They weren't Shakers; they had no excuse to stay self-contained. It wasn't as though Emily forced herself on them, either. She had no desire to understand all their private jokes or obscure Magatuck references. She didn't particularly want to know about the math teacher who had committed suicide their senior year, or about the collage they had cut from various magazines for Lisa's sweet-sixteen party: "I Can't Believe I Ate the Whole Thing!" "You've Come a Long Way, Baby!" Emily had her own history, and God knew she didn't want theirs.

Emily never did come to another dinner at the Lucky Wok, although she continued to take part in lesser events. One afternoon she accompanied Ann and Lisa to the studio to watch Meredith shoot her weekly segment on "Consumer Watch." They sat on folding chairs against the wall of the studio as Meredith stood on the set behind a table that was covered with toys. Meredith was highly groomed in TV readywear, her hair a touch too stiff, a full bow at her throat. The lights were on her, making all her surfaces bright and shadowless. Meredith's skin appeared as pure as good stationery. She was all grace as she stood in front of a small table, holding up a doll.

". . . but perhaps the most outrageous of all," said Meredith, "is an offering from Selden Toys, the Little Paco doll. Little Paco comes with a wide sombrero, no shirt and no shoes, his hand outstretched as if to suggest begging." The camera closed in on Little Paco so that the doll's face could be seen from an inch away: the nominally Latino features, the caramel skin, the painted-on, ridged black hair. "Not only does this doll promote ethnic stereotypes," Meredith continued, "it's also unsafe. Included are three 'authentic Mexican pesos,' which can be easily swallowed and choked on by young children. Need I say more? I'm Meredith Grey, and that's all for today."

How different this was from high school, when Meredith had starred in *Long Day's Journey into Night,* and had unknowingly given Mrs. Tyrone a subtle Long Island accent. Gone was the fifteen-year-old girl who had stood on the stage of Magatuck High, pretending to be a deranged, middle-aged dope addict. After the play, Meredith had been surrounded backstage by friends and parents and teachers, who told her she was brilliant, and all night at the cast party, held in the paneled rec room of the asthmatic boy playing Mr. Tyrone, Meredith had held court. Lisa had been the props manager for the play, and everyone had told her she had done a wonderful job with the gloomy confines of the Tyrone home. Ann had appeared in the play in the role of "Cathleen," a servant to Meredith. It was a tiny part, and Ann performed it well, but nobody could think about anyone but Meredith. And this, so many years later, had not changed. "She makes me sick," Ann said as they sat waiting for Meredith to remove her TV makeup and reappear. "God gave her everything: looks, talent, success. And now he's put her on TV. What's left for the rest of us?"

"Kindness to animals," said Emily. "I don't think that's been taken."

"Well, I'm happy for her," Lisa said. "I think she could be the next Diane Sawyer."

"If that happened," said Ann, "I would have to shoot myself. No, a gun wouldn't be violent enough. I would have to do that Mishima thing. Disembowel myself with a Ginsu knife."

"I still don't see why she had to change her name," said Lisa. "What was wrong with Guzzi?"

And they all had a good, mean laugh at Meredith's expense.

Lately, Lisa had begun to notice that she looked different when she stepped out of the shower in the morning. Her body had become a little fleshier, and her flesh a little rosier. This, she decided, was what marriage did to you. Ann had become a lesbian and evolved into a cool, sleek whippet, while Lisa had become a married woman and was in serious danger of devolving into her mother, with wide hips and a wedding band, and a sudden show of interest from her female relatives, who felt that she had finally joined them in this society of indentured wives.

She had kept her maiden name, on principle, even though Zinn was far better than Vopilska. Once in a while, when she was asked her name at the dry cleaners, or when making dinner reservations, she would give Eric's name just for the weird kick of it. "Zinn" seemed to be a password to some other life. "Zinn" was so easy to spell, too: a short, zippy name, vastly different from her own homely and seemingly random collection of letters.

When she first eased into the World of Zinn, Lisa became less accessible to Meredith and Ann. As a newly married couple, the Vopilska-Zinns were always in demand, giving guest appearances at Zinn family gatherings, or showing up to watch a slideshow of Lisa's aunt's trip to Tibet. Whenever they had a little free time, they would turn to each other, nod, and head for bed. The sex remained wonderful, got better in fact, and Lisa felt secretly proud of herself that she was so free sexually. Sometimes, when they were making love, the telephone rang and rang, and the machine picked it up. The recorded message would be followed by Meredith or Ann speaking self-consciously into the answering machine, saying, "Lisa? Eric? Hey, kids. Are you there?" Then the voice would pause, and sometimes Lisa wanted to leap out of bed to get the phone, but before she did, she would look at Eric and see that he was waiting to see what she would choose. *Me or them,* he was thinking. *Pick one.* So Lisa chose him, and stayed in bed, listening to the clunking of Meredith or Ann hanging up the telephone. She wished she could be on the telephone with her friends *and* nuzzling Eric; she wished that being married meant you could have everyone you loved all around you, and that your home could be a kind of drop-in center, with the door always swinging wide to welcome guests.

But marriage was nothing like that. She lived with Eric in her same hospital high-rise apartment that was now overstuffed with wedding gifts: spun-glass vases, cheerily painted Mexican pottery, coffeemakers from many lands. There was even a huge rubber tree standing by the terrace doors, its leaves casting huge, ominous spider shadows. Sometimes Lisa would get up in the middle of the night for a glass of water, and as she made her way through the dark apartment with all its objects and shadows, she felt that she was in a stranger's house. What *was* this place? And who were these two people who lived here? One of them had gained all this weight, and the other was a sudden dermatologist.

But it wasn't just them.

Ann had changed, too; over the past year she had gone from the porcupine look to an unflattering androgynous teen-idol look, finally ending up as a lesbian, looking better than she ever had in her life, with blunt-cut chin-length hair that swung nicely when she turned her head, and great clothes that she borrowed from Emily.

But Meredith was the one who seemed to have changed the most. Lisa may have become married, and heavier, and less available, but Meredith had become famous. Sort of. At least, she *looked* like someone who was famous. People glanced at her with curiosity on the street, trying to remember where they had seen this pretty young professional woman. Ever since she had started appearing on "Consumer Watch," she began looking like someone who belonged on TV. She dressed older and brighter: blazers, little scarves, antique pins. Her voice became throatier and more confident. Every morning, Meredith read four newspapers, as though there was going to be a quiz on current events and she was afraid she might fail. She worked out furiously at a private gym with a hulking young trainer named Wilfredo. She went to a nutritionist who took samples of her hair and skin and blood, and told her that if she ever wanted to get anywhere in this life, she needed to bombard her system with zinc. "Zinc, zinc, zinc!" the nutritionist called out as she left his office, and Meredith dutifully swallowed horse-sized nuggets of zinc every morning as she pored over the *Wall Street Journal*. Meredith was clearly on her way up; this stint on public TV was just a way station before she was claimed by the evening news, or by one of those morning shows where the set looks like somebody's Early American living room, complete with a couch covered with hard little needlepoint pillows. It was impossible to keep up with Meredith, so Lisa didn't even try.

It seemed to all their friends that Lisa and Eric were happy. The appearance of happiness was a helpful thing; Lisa would have been mortified if anyone knew the ideas she had sometimes, the insulting thoughts about Eric that would have crushed him if he'd been able to read her mind. She came home from dinner at the Lucky Wok one night, feeling cranky in a way that she hardly understood. When she walked in, the apartment struck her all over again as absurdly overstuffed, like one of those grotesque deli sandwiches that you can't even get your mouth around, and can't really enjoy. Eric had cleared a space for himself on the couch and was lying down, reading a magazine. Lisa came over and bent down to kiss him, then she plopped down in the armchair beside the rubber tree. Idly she reached out to touch the leaves; one snapped off in her hand. It was brown and crisp as a potato chip.

"I don't know why we have this plant," Lisa said. "We never water it. We're totally negligent parents."

"So throw it out," said Eric, now looking up from his book.

"It was a wedding present, remember?" said Lisa. "From your parents' friends the Bittermans. We can't just throw it out. Besides, what would I do, just dump it off the terrace so it could fall sixteen floors and kill the doorman?"

"Whatever you want, Lisa," said Eric.

"You aren't even listening," she said.

"I'm trying to read," said Eric.

She peered at what he was reading. "Ah, *Contemporary*

Dermatological Equipment," she said. "I hear it's overwritten, though quite moving in parts."

"Uncle Mort says that when you're just starting out," said Eric, "it really pays to order high-quality stuff. State of the art."

"I'm trying to talk to you about this rubber tree, Eric," said Lisa.

"Okay, okay," he said with a sigh. "I'm all yours." He pointedly closed the magazine and put it on the coffee table, between a trapezoidal Danish glass ashtray and three veined marble eggs that sat in their own little nest, wedding presents all.

"I think it's a metaphor for our marriage," said Lisa.

"A rubber tree is a metaphor for our marriage?" said Eric. "Where'd you get that idea? Did Meredith and Ann cook it up?"

"This has nothing to do with them," said Lisa. "You always blame my friends whenever you and I have a fight."

"All right, I'm sorry," he said. "Please tell me why a rubber tree is a metaphor for our marriage."

"Well," Lisa began, "because it was a wedding present. I read this O. Henry story when I was a kid; it was about this girl who gets really, really sick, and every day she lies in bed and looks outside her window. It's winter, and there's a vine growing on the wall, and she gets it into her head that when the last leaf falls off the vine she'll die. She tells this to everybody, including this old man who's an artist and lives upstairs. One night there's a terrible storm, and there's no way in the world that the last leaf could have made it through the storm, and everybody is terrified to open the curtains and let her see outside. But she insists, and when they look, they see that the last leaf is still there, clinging to the vine. Somehow it made it all the way through the storm, so now she knows she's going to get well. But what she doesn't know is that it isn't real; the man just *painted* this leaf on the wall in the middle of the night, in order to give her hope. But the O. Henry twist is that he caught pneumonia while he was out painting in the cold and died." Having finished her story, Lisa sat back in the chair with her arms folded, looking at Eric.

But all he said was, "What's your point?"

"I'm not sure it's a single point," said Lisa with a little less certainty, "but I think we're letting things die a little."

"What things?" he asked.

"Our marriage," she said.

"Okay, fine," said Eric. "When the last leaf falls off this crummy rubber tree, then our marriage is over."

"Fine," said Lisa.

Eric put his hands over his eyes and rubbed them like a sleepy child. "Why," he said, "couldn't the Bittermans have given us a wok?"

Later that night, lying in bed together, their bodies twisted around each other yet absurdly relaxed, Lisa thought about the first time they had ever had sex, in the tiny cubicle at the hospital. Even though they had both been in uniform—she in her green scrubs, he in his plain white coat just like any other doctor or waiter or ice cream vendor—somehow they had managed to single each other out, to choose each other from the masses. Now she looked over at him as his face slackened into sleep. His mouth was open, and she saw a little puddle of drool start to collect and widen on the sheet. If she were to meet Eric now, would she fall in love with him? If, on their first date, he told her that old people really depressed him, and that

104

he preferred to tend to the pustules on the foreheads and chins of sullen teenagers from New York private schools, would she still think he was the one for her? Lately, he seemed to want to forget everything he knew from his work in gerontology. "So I'm scared of getting old," he had said to Lisa one night in bed. "Don't hate me for it."

So she didn't. She continued to love him in that dumb, essentially human way that kept their limbs entwined and their faces close. She still thought about the fact that both of their names were on the mailbox downstairs. L. VOPIL-SKA/E. ZINN, the label read, as though carved inside a heart on a tree. Married love was something that she had over both Ann and Meredith. Exalted, official, licensed love. She had it, and they didn't. This fact pleased her immensely, and as soon as she realized this, she felt ashamed. Was she a terrible person? She wished her friends well, certainly. She wanted them both to have whatever it was they wanted in the world. But for now, she had the corner on the married life. Lisa moved closer to Eric, and placed her cheek by his. It took her only a second to realize she was lying right on the wet spot.

ight

eredith was turning thirty soon, and no one would give her any sympathy. No one understood what thirty meant to someone like Meredith. No one understood that she was the kind of woman who was supposed to have been deeply entrenched in the specifics of love by this point, so that when thirty arrived, with its big three and its big fat zero rolling like boulders into her life, she would be ready.

But she wasn't ready at all. She was frightened, and for the first time ever, she worried that she would never meet a man she could tolerate for very long, and that her specialness and loveliness would start to recede, and that she, who had always been so exciting to men, would somehow be left behind. The ordinary-looking, meek women of the world would rise up and find great happiness, but not Meredith. She decided that she would make the best of it, and would throw herself into her work, but then she remembered that a woman who is unloved for very long probably becomes desperate and unappealing, neither of which makes for a very telegenic appearance.

She would have to give up her TV show eventually. She would disappear from the public eye, moving to a town in upstate New York and opening a knickknack shop, the kind of place that sells homemade fudge and little dolls carved out of local apples.

Alone in bed at night, Meredith began to review her entire sexual history, like someone picking at a scab. It was upsetting to remember the various men she had been to bed with over the years, yet it was also a comfort to be reminded of all the men who had ever desired her. She had always prided herself on her sexual skills and absence of inhibitions. From the moment an elderly, Parkinsonian gynecologist had fitted sixteen-year-old Meredith with a diaphragm, she had been sexually unafraid. The diaphragm became a kind of amulet that would carry her through life. In the beginning, the boys were all rotten lovers: zealous premature-ejaculators, but still Meredith forged ahead.

Now, as she was about to turn thirty, she looked back over her sexual history like Will and Ariel Durant, trying to neatly frame each passionate or misguided moment. There were so many men to remember: the puppyish ones in the beginning, then the slightly menacing James Dean knockoffs she favored later on. There was John Staley in college, and then, after graduation, a series of trim young bankers and lawyers in Armani suits. There was the man behind the counter at More, Please, that suffocatingly cute take-out gourmet place on Madison Avenue. He had spooned tarragon turkey salad into a container for her and gazed across the scale with a smirk on his angular face, and she had agreed to give him her telephone number. In bed he continued to be angular and gorgeous, but she had to break the relationship off when

108

he tried to involve her in a pyramid scheme. Then, of course, there was Alan. Although she had been out with many men since then, she still missed him, and sometimes when they passed each other in the halls, at the station, they threw each other tortured glances, like star-crossed teenagers. Recently she had seen him at the drinking fountain on the eighth floor, stooping down to meet the flow of lukewarm water, and she was reminded of the way he used to crane his neck down awkwardly to look at her during sex.

Counting men was like counting sheep, except it only made Meredith more anxious and awake. At some point during the night, it occurred to her that she had slept with so many men that she might be HIV-positive. The thought had occurred to her before, but usually during daylight hours, and she was always able to dismiss her worries as self-indulgent neuroses. But now, having just completed a middle-of-the-night roll call of every man she had ever fucked, she was seized by renewed terror. She had to admit that there were times in the past when the man hadn't worn a condom. In the early years, before anyone had ever heard of AIDS, it hadn't been necessary, but later on, she still sometimes couldn't bear to send a man fumbling in his wallet for a little square of tinfoil, or, worse, out in the driving rain to a Wal-Mart in the middle of the night with an erection poking against the fabric of his pants.

Now if she concentrated hard enough, she could almost feel the virus percolating in her blood. She saw herself in five years, the host of a magazine-format TV show, famous and respected and with really great hair, when suddenly the virus's hibernation would end. She indulged in thoughts of her own funeral, doing a quick head-count of the mourners, trying to determine how well she had been loved, and whether or not Diane Sawyer was there.

Meredith had always possessed an unerring capacity for self-dramatization; when she was a child and her father had taken a business trip to Toledo, she imagined his airplane exploding, and Meredith and her family standing stately but stricken at the funeral. She pictured her little brother stepping forward to do a John-John Kennedy salute as the coffin carrying the body of Lawrence J. Guzzi was carried by. But her father hadn't died; he was still a CPA in Magatuck, and in fact, Meredith's life had been largely untouched by death.

But now she was certain her good luck was coming to an end. What had Meredith been thinking of, all these years? Her body had been covered with fingerprints, her insides had been plumbed by self-important men, by pretty men, by stupid men. Her sexual history was starting to look like a horror story, ending with Meredith lying in a coffin, Diane Sawyer weeping discreetly nearby.

Reflexively, Meredith began to pray. *Dear God,* she thought, *please spare me.* Then she added, as she had always done in these middle-of-the-night bargaining moments, *I will do anything.* What kind of a God did she think this was, anyway? One who could be bribed? A shady character in clashing plaids, hanging around an OTB storefront all day? No, he could certainly not be bribed or blackmailed or expected to believe the desperate pleas of a woman who went to church only rarely, and who had been sexually involved with many, many men, including one who was married. He would take one look at this creature cowering pathetically in the darkness and know she was only using him for personal gain.

Meredith was not a spiritual person, and she knew she would probably never be one. Her family had celebrated all the major Christian holidays and had occasionally taken the kids to church for folk mass, which Meredith had always loved because it featured guitar-playing teen-aged boys with longish hair and clean, even teeth, singing well-enunciated versions of Bob Dylan songs. Although she was not spiritual, she still liked to think of herself as a Christian; the word had such a soothing sound to it. She sometimes went to a church in the West 70s, a small, undistinguished place with an active soup kitchen for the homeless in the basement. Once Meredith had spent a Saturday afternoon there doling out food, none of which happened to be soup. The homeless men and women had been very grateful, and had said thank-you and stacked their own plates when they were done eating. Meredith had liked the idea of being charitable, but after a few hours the heat of the basement and the smells of stew and industrial cleanser had depressed her terribly. When they asked her back for the following Saturday, she had said she was busy, and so they never asked her again. She was embarrassed at her behavior, and to make up for it she had immediately gone out and made a big donation to a homeless shelter. Lisa, she knew, would have been in that soup kitchen week after week, arriving in time to set up, then dispensing the food and staying around afterward for the entire clean-up. Lisa would have been the one in pink rubber gloves, her arms plunged into a sink of dishwater. She would have worked all day, and then would have been the last one out of the basement, the one whose job it was to shut off the lights.

Dear God, Meredith thought now, *I am so ashamed of myself.* The emotion was pure, the moment tender, and she might have left it like that, but she couldn't help adding a favor for herself: *Please let me be HIV-negative.* This was the lowest form of prayer imaginable. *I'll do anything,* she thought again. But God, unlike men, didn't seem to want anything from her.

So Meredith called Lisa.

She lifted the telephone from its cradle in the dark room, and punched the greenly lit buttons of Lisa's number. The phone rang twice, then Lisa answered. It was three in the morning, but Lisa was so accustomed to late-night calls from the hospital that she was able to sound as though she had just been sitting, wide-awake, beside the phone, waiting for it to ring.

"Lisa, it's me," said Meredith. "I'm really sorry to call, but I've been having a panic attack. Don't laugh at me, but I think I'm HIV-positive."

There was a long sigh. "Meredith," said Lisa, "we've been through this before. You are probably not infected. Were you involved with someone who falls into a risk category?"

Meredith thought about this. "There was this one guy, who I met at a party," she said. "I think he might have been bisexual. He insisted we stay up to watch the late movie on TV, which happened to be *Spartacus.*"

"I think you're overreacting," said Lisa. "But if it will make you feel better, why don't you come by my office tomorrow morning and I'll give you a blood test."

"Thank you," said Meredith. "You're the best."

"And in the future," said Lisa, "you should definitely make the man wear a condom."

"I wish I could make him wear an oven mitt," said Meredith, and then they said goodnight.

Thank God for Lisa, Meredith thought. What did

people do if they didn't have Lisa in their life? When Meredith hung up the telephone she felt confident that she was healthy. She would go for the blood test tomorrow (it would be too embarrassing not to), and it would turn out negative, and her AIDS fear would become simply another deeply felt, then instantly forgotten anxiety.

She thought about Lisa lying in bed with Eric, pressed against him. God, he was awful, but she had to admit that there was something to be said for not being alone. She started thinking of everyone she knew lying in bed with his or her lover: her mother and father, Alan and his wife, Ann and Emily. *Ann and Emily.* The idea of being in bed with another woman was still baffling and a little sordid to Meredith.

Ever since Ann's announcement, Meredith had tried to picture Ann kissing and touching Emily the way she would a man. The question in Meredith's mind wasn't "What do lesbians do?" but, rather, *"Why* do lesbians do it?" Was there something embedded in Ann's genetic makeup that had led her to this place, of all places? Or was it environmental? Of course, the nature versus nurture debate was a popular one these days, and "The Last Word" occasionally dragged out earnest neurobiologists and Pentacostal ministers who spoke in tongues, putting them around a table so they could fight.

Meredith knew that she still wasn't ready to go to sleep, so she turned on her light and walked to her bookshelves, searching until she found her battered paperback edition of *The Group.* Then she lay in bed and leafed through the pages. The passage that concerned her was toward the very end of the book: *"Studying Lakey with the customs man, they asked themselves, in silence, how long Lakey had*

*been a Lesbian, whether the Baroness had made her one or she
had started on her own. This led them to wonder whether she
could possibly have been one at college—suppressed, of
course."*

The more Meredith thought about it, the more Ann's
entire life seemed to be a syndrome heading inevitably
toward this moment of revelation: the proliferation of gay
male friends in college, the insistence on unflattering haircuts, the continually disappointing sex with men. *Of
course, of course,* Meredith thought, and yet she, the sexual cosmopolite of the three, was still shocked. She started
thinking about the role that she and Lisa might have
played in Ann's sexual formation, and it occurred to her
that perhaps the phenomenon of MerLisAn had created
such a cozy harbor of female friendship that no man could
ever be as good. Maybe Meredith and Lisa had been too
nice, too nurturing, and Ann just wanted to re-create that
experience forever. *It's our fault,* Meredith thought, then
she inwardly chided herself for thinking of lesbianism as
a liability. No, she told herself, it's just another lifestyle
option, like becoming a Rastafarian, or deciding, midlife,
to quit a prestigious law firm and attend clown college.

Meredith couldn't imagine gazing at another woman
with longing. With men, you wanted to be all over them,
figuring out their strange, dark natures, making their mus-
cled bodies go limp and their mouths open like baby
birds. In bed, men fell in love with Meredith; she could
watch it happen, slow motion. Their eyes became heavy,
their voices a rasp. She liked to straddle them so she could
see the predictable amalgam of pleasure and gratitude on
their faces. She also secretly liked to admire the way her
own breasts looked in moonlight. But what would you do
in bed with a woman? Gossip? When she really thought

about lesbians having sex, she felt an inner shudder. The truth was that she *didn't* want to think about it; she *didn't* want to picture them in bed. The most she could force herself to imagine was two women wearing Lanz nightgowns, hugging a lot, and reading aloud from the journals of Anaïs Nin.

When she returned *The Group* to her bookshelf, she noticed *Middlemarch* on the shelf beneath it. Poor, neglected *Middlemarch,* begun so many times, only to be returned to its place, unread. It was as though she had a bad relationship with this great novel, as though, no matter how many times they dated, conversation was always forced, and they each went home alone. She pulled it from the shelf now and began it again. *"Miss Brooke had that kind of beauty which seems to be thrown into relief by poor dress,"* she read, and the familiar words were comforting to her. She knew them by heart, the way she knew the Pledge of Allegiance, or the opening lines of "Stopping by Woods on a Snowy Evening." I know what I'll do, she told herself: I'll sit here all night and read this thing. I'll read it until my eyes grow achy and dry. I'll read it until I start to squint, like Ann, but I'll never get glasses; I'll get soft contact lenses. Tinted. Azure, like the Mediterranean. I'll read this goddamn book until I've reached the last page, and then I'll never have to crack it open again.

But once again, the elegant stream of words bounced right off Meredith, was refracted, dodged, left scattered. Even Ann, the bona fide intellectual, had probably not been sitting home reading a book tonight. She had probably gone out somewhere with Emily, dancing together in the heat of a women's bar, hipbones bumping, or maybe she was hunched over a big piece of oaktag, painting a sign for some upcoming march on Washington, and now, in the middle of the night, she was fast asleep in Emily's arms. Ann was part of a group now; in a way, all lesbians and gay men had become Ann's siblings, or at least that was what she liked to say. Even Lisa, with that inappropriate husband of hers, had a family.

But why, Meredith asked herself, do *I* have to sit here alone tonight? There were scores of men who wanted to take her out to dinner, to a movie, to an inn for the weekend. But when she thought about getting up and getting ready for an evening out, she realized that she no longer had the patience for it. What was the point? She was getting too old to keep doing this. She would be turning thirty soon. Meredith Grey, *née* Guzzi, was actually turning thirty! The thought of it depressed her beyond belief. As a teenager, she had seen herself as sophisticated and capable, and after her adolescence ended, she had seen herself as a young and stylish career woman in New York. It had barely occurred to her that thirty would arrive and she would still be unattached and adrift. She barely had the energy to go out on dates anymore.

Just the other night, she had gone to dinner with a man named Jeffrey Bliss. He was very attractive in a generic young architect way, but she thought she could manage him and that it might be gratifying, later, to open the buttons on his shirt and get a look at the hard, furred chest underneath. When he asked her back to his apartment after the restaurant she went, and a little while later, sitting on his couch with something predictable on the CD player—she thought it was the "Death in Venice" movement from that Mahler symphony—he turned to her and said, "Meredith, do you want to?"

"Do I want to *what*?" she asked.

"You know," Jeffrey said, and he made a circle with his fingers, then poked the index finger on his other hand through the circle, in the international sign for fucking. It was like *Children of a Lesser God.* Meredith was so taken aback by his vulgarity, by the fact that he couldn't say the words "make love," or "go to bed with me," or some acceptable synonym, that she stormed out of his apartment, and he didn't even try to follow her. She thought he should at least have followed her.

She had the best, most pleasurable, and stupidest job in the world, and despite her complaints to Ann and Lisa, it actually did pay pretty well. Soon she would become coproducer, and her salary would be increased considerably. She had begun to think of buying an apartment, leaving this studio behind and sleeping on a real bed in a real bedroom, preferably beside a real man who wasn't a loser or a shit, who didn't have to leave in an hour, and who wasn't threatened by the amazing trajectory of her career.

Maybe I should become a lesbian, too, she thought for a moment with some humor. *Oh, darling, do that again, but slowly,* she imagined saying to another woman, and she started to laugh. No, she would never experience a sudden sea change and become a lesbian, even if there were no men left on earth. Even if she was mistakenly accused of a crime and sent to prison for life, she would never become some woman's squeeze. Instead, released from the world of men and their strange hulking ways, their circus bear attempts at being civilized, their dark odors, their transparent lies, their broad chests, their inadequately furnished apartments, their empty refrigerators, their massive tie collections, their idiotic charm—she would give it all up forever. Instead, she would curl up on

ine

When Emily moved in with Ann, Adele Rogoff had gone off with Ann's father to Las Vegas for three days, even though neither of them liked to gamble and Ann's father hated to fly. They simply had to go somewhere, do something, to escape the fact that their daughter was setting up house with another woman, one who couldn't be hidden from the relatives at the Rogoff family barbecues, which seemed to take place every Sunday. They weren't a close family, the Rogoffs, but they liked to use their Weber grills every chance they could. The news of Ann and Emily would not be taken lightly. It would circulate among all the women in the family, just as the news of cousin Sharon Rogoff's conversion to Catholicism had circulated, not to mention cousin Adam Rogoff's failure, for the third consecutive time, to pass the New York State bar exam. Soon it would be everywhere, with Ann showing up at these family gatherings with Emily on her arm, the two women schmoozing happily on some aunt and uncle's lawn, the barbecue sizzling fragrantly and sending up smoke signals into the sky: A ROGOFF GIRL HAS BECOME A LESBIAN. Most of the relatives would insist that the family had never had a lesbian among them before, although some had always wondered about second-cousin Miriam in Toledo, who had long ago run away from her marriage to join the WACS, and had never come home.

Now Adele and Herb Rogoff were standing at the one-armed bandits in Vegas, pulling levers and chucking in quarters from a plastic bucket, trying to forget. Ann only wanted to remember. She wanted all of this to register with her forever: the way it felt to be this age, living in this massive city and having a woman lover. She hoped she never forgot any of it. These thoughts of forgetting made Emily suspicious. "I mean, how could you forget?" Emily asked. "I'll always be here. I'm not going anywhere."

But Ann wasn't so certain. She didn't trust love, and she didn't, finally, trust Emily, who had been in love many times already, and she wasn't even thirty. How could a woman who had told others she was in love with them, and who had moved her stationary bicycle into other apartments, other homes, be trusted? Emily loved deeply, and passionately, in the grand style of old 1940s movies, but with a twist. She admitted that she liked turning women "queer," as she called it, or at least bringing this fact out in them, shaming them into the truth with her own beauty and wit. But it wasn't just Emily who had done this to Ann. The groundwork had been laid years earlier. Possibly, according to articles, in the womb. Back in 1962, while Adele Rogoff was vomiting into a toilet and shopping for smocklike blouses, maybe the first shoots of homosexuality were poking up within the shrimplike embryo inside her, the chemicals swirling in that tender new brain stem, the genes doing their little waltz, the twisted double helix of DNA creating a ladder to be climbed toward other women, or a ladder that other women could climb to reach Ann's elevated bed.

Or maybe it wasn't nature after all, it was nurture. Ann thought about her parents. True, her mother was pushy and her father was passive, but so what? That was true for almost everyone she knew. The fathers were a passive herd, or at least seemed that way, because they were never home, spending their days in the city, returning home at night on the railroad to spend a few hours of darkness before bedtime with the children they barely knew. So what if she had to vie with the newspaper for his attention? She had loved sitting in his gray Banlon-suited lap, the financial page crackling against her, his knee jiggling in a vague approximation of a horsey ride to keep her happy as he studied the Dow. Her father had been remote but pleasant, and her mother had been a live wire who made salads in the shapes of a girl's face to please Ann: olives for eyes, a radish nose, a flat carrot stick line for a mouth, and lettuce leaves fanning out for hair. Maybe Ann had been attracted to the salad girl; maybe she had longed to place her lips against the cool orange line of that carrot-stick mouth. Who knew anymore? The early sprouting of her sexuality had become little more than a rumor now. Whatever she had become had long been finished and set in bronze. That was why late-in-life lesbianism was such an embarrassment. It forced you to reenact the early stirrings of sex, the adolescent gawking at the fact that the self can do these things, or even wants to. But her whole history had taken on a different cast now.

She thought of the younger girl who had lived around

the corner in Magatuck: Tammy Granucci, who was so dumb and so compliant that Ann had never thought to introduce her to either Lisa or Meredith. What use would either of them have had for this little girl in the house with the oil painting of a sad balladeer over the Rococo living-room couch? One afternoon, when Tammy's parents were at work at the discount children's clothing store they owned, SalGrans (for the father, Salvador Granucci), Ann and Tammy took two plates of Sno Balls, those flesh-soft, hot-pink domed pastries, and two glasses of milk, and had a snack on the plastic-covered couch. When they were done, with coconut flakes still clinging to their lips, they started to wrestle, which was something Ann had begun to enjoy. They wrestled in some clumsy girlish way, yet she felt as though they were bear cubs, and a certain energy was awakened in her, and apparently in Tammy, too, for they tore at each other like enemies. Tammy tugged at Ann's skort until it was pulled down to her knees. *Skort.* The term referred to a brief fashion trend of Ann's childhood—half skirt, half shorts, just another entry under the blurred rubric of bad-taste 1960s clothes that had since disappeared off the face of the earth. Suddenly Ann jumped to her feet and said to Tammy, "Let's play Queen and Slave."

Tammy looked at her with her uncomprehending, obedient face, and when Ann asked her to fetch something they could use as whips, Tammy went downstairs to her father's workbench and brought back two dowels that had been meant to stir paint. Ann whipped at that poor girl, breathlessly muttering, "I'm the Queen," as she struck her. "I'm the Queen, so I'm gonna have to punish you," she said. Tammy allowed the stick to slap against her bare legs, and her face assumed a closed, unreadable expression. Pleasure? Humiliation? She was not an expressive girl—and she was in the lowest reading group at school—and this might have gone on for hours, but finally, out of a sense of courtesy, for after all, this was Tammy's living room, Ann decided it was only fair to let Tammy be the Queen, too. "Here," she said, with magnanimity, passing her the dowel. "It's your turn."

To Ann's disappointment, the other girl didn't take the dowel and proceed to whip her back. Instead, Tammy only brandished it like a scepter, mumbling, "I'm a Queen. But see, I'm a nice Queen. Chocolate ice cream for everybody!" Which kind of took all the fun out of it. But the whipping, and the wrestling they had done earlier, and the two matching bodies rolling on the white carpet, Ann had to have known that was about sex. Even Tammy Granucci had to have known. It was just that no one was allowed to say it. A few minutes later, when they heard Tammy's parents' car arriving home from SalGran's, Tammy quickly stood up and smoothed down her blouse and screamed violently at Ann to pull up her skort. And a few days later, when Ann asked Tammy if she could come over and play Queen and Slave again, Tammy had looked distinctly uncomfortable and said no, she had to help her parents with inventory at the store.

But now, almost twenty years later, being a lesbian was the hottest ticket in town. Lesbians had been written into the plots of soap operas; lesbians were on the cover of weekly newsmagazines. Photogenic ones only, of course: a wheaten-haired couple with their wheaten-haired turkey-baster son, fighting the PTA and apparently winning. For once, Ann felt as though she was on the inside of something important. She had spent her life watching Meredith traipse off with men, and knew that she could have whichever men she chose. Meredith had access to things, and Ann did not. But suddenly she was on the inside of this swelling, vocal movement, where she was right at home among bull dykes and models and grandmothers with walkers. She went with Emily to the Gay Pride March, their arms locked, looking great in tank tops, shoulders getting sunburned as they walked down Fifth Avenue. They marched with other women, and they also marched with men. But oh, the men. So many of them were dropping dead, and yet they marched anyway. Raggedy thin guys in jeans that were falling off their hips, with hollowed faces like an El Greco. Emily's ex-roommate Lloyd was HIV-positive, and he had turned Emily, and now Ann, into an AIDS activist.

It was a relief to think about something other than yourself for at least a few minutes each day, Ann decided. Having a political life swept you right outside the boring confines of your own body, with its petty needs and history and failings. Ann and Emily went with Lloyd to a protest at a pharmaceutical company, and at a hospital, and once, they even went down to Washington to the National Institutes of Health, where they lay down on the road and pretended to be dead. Meredith would never be caught dead pretending to be dead. *I am a better person than Meredith,* Ann thought with some satisfaction as she lay on her back that day and stared up at the Bethesda sky. Ann felt as though she had a cause—homosexuality and all its trappings, in sickness and in health—and she was happy to be part of it, but she didn't know if a cause could last forever.

They held an open house when Emily moved in. Several people had the idea to bring plants, among them a cactus, with a fat, swollen bulb and little protuberances, a private joke, perhaps, that phalluses should be forced on these women who refused them otherwise. There were plants and also a set of pot holders with details from paintings on them (one of the pot holders was badly singed on a roasting pan months later, obliterating the entire left side of Jane Avril's face). Another lesbian couple, with the Biblical names of Naomi and Ruth, brought a deadly boring CD of hammer dulcimer music, which Emily instantly put on, and which threatened to turn the party into an afternoon at the Cloisters; all they needed were the Unicorn tapestries.

Lisa arrived with Eric in tow, and Ann almost felt sorry for him. She had never seen someone looking so unhappy to be at a party, someone so unwilling to be where he was. She imagined him wearing a T-shirt that read I'D RATHER BE . . . but when she came to the end of the slogan, she couldn't imagine what it should say. Eric didn't seem to have many interests, not that she had ever drawn him out to try to figure out what they were. "I'd Rather Be . . ." she started, and then she finished the thought with "Removing an Unsightly Mole."

This really wasn't fair of her, she thought, looking at him sitting so uneasily on her couch in this small, crowded apartment. He swiped the point of a corn chip through some salsa and ate it, then peered at his watch, as though that simple action of dipping and eating a chip might have made time pass considerably. His beeper was attached to his thick belt. She didn't know that dermatologists carried beepers. Did they really get skin emergencies? she wondered. Maybe actresses or models suddenly broke out in acne or hives before a big shoot and needed emergency care. She knew that he would be immensely relieved if his beeper went off and he could summon up a reason to leave the party, or even just go call his service on the kitchen phone. Eric needed to be doing something, to be midmotion, and here at this party given by two lesbians, he had absolutely nothing to do. Eric's beeper remained silent. The only beeping came from Lloyd's watch, which let him know it was time to take his AZT, which he swallowed with a glass of Snapple.

Meredith arrived toward the end of the party. As usual, her arrival was a big deal, and there was a small stir among the crowd, and someone whispered to someone else, "Isn't that that woman from public TV?" The whisper was just loud enough for Meredith to hear it, and this probably made her day. Oh, the joy of being recognized! Ann thought about Harry's young authors at work, who responded to their own names with great pleasure. Their names became a tropism; they turned toward the healing light. Now Meredith waded right into the party as though she were at ease, which Ann knew she was not. She was in Ann's territory, which must have certainly made her as uncomfortable as the Queen of England visiting a leper colony.

Meredith had brought a prism as a gift. It came from one of those expensive little craft-boutiques on Columbus Avenue, and you were supposed to hang it in your window and everyone was supposed to ooh and ah over the splashing of colors around your room. Personally, Ann had always thought refracted sunlight was overrated, but she acted pleased and put it in the pile with all the other gifts.

Everything was humming along pleasantly enough, when Ann realized that an argument was starting in the doorway to the kitchen. Eric and Naomi had squared off and were really going at it. "Let me explain something to you," Eric was saying. "If you want to be treated with non-Western medicine, that's your prerogative. But to tell me that what I do is patriarchal and unsafe is just patently untrue, and I resent it."

"Western medicine," Naomi said, "is based on the subjugation of women, just like Western society. Women are natural healers, and they always have been. We work with herbs," she said, pronouncing the *h*. "We have a lot of innate knowledge."

"Nobody has innate knowledge of medicine," said Eric. "You have to go to medical school, okay? You have to study a lot. You have to stay up all night and work with patients. You're not born with it."

"You and your kind have been controlling women's lives throughout history," said Naomi calmly.

"Oh, tell me about it," said Eric.

"What about all the unnecessary hysterectomies that you perform each year?" Naomi said.

"That *I* perform?" said Eric. "Oh, right, I'm the hysterectomy king, aren't I?" He sneered. "In case you forgot," he said, "I happen to be a dermatologist."

The hammer-dulcimer music played soothingly on, but everyone stopped their own conversations to listen to the argument, which wound down into unhappy silence. A moment later, Eric excused himself and made his way over to where Lisa was standing. He whispered to her, "I'm leaving."

"Are you sure?" she said.

"I have work to do," he said. "I want to get home. You can stay if you want."

But of course she didn't stay. For Lisa, marriage meant that when your spouse wanted to leave, you left, too. You were joined at the hip, no matter what happened. Even if your spouse had just embarrassed you, had been boorish or unpleasant or dyspeptic, when he said he wanted to leave, you grabbed your coat and left. If Emily had announced that she was leaving a party, would Ann feel that same compulsion to follow? She looked across at Emily, who was laughing as she told some law school anecdote, and she realized that she had no idea.

Later, when the other guests had gone and Ann and Emily were cleaning up, they somehow found themselves in the middle of their own argument. It began with a benign discussion of Eric. Both Ann and Emily saw Eric as enraged and harmless, like a beetle on its back, hairy legs flailing. "He was so defensive," Emily was saying as she dumped the ashes from Ruth's Gauloises into the toilet. "Naomi can be really obnoxious, but Eric took it personally. He's really spooked by strong women."

"Why do you consider Naomi a strong woman?" Ann asked. "Just because she's loud?"

"No, because she has strong convictions," said Emily. "Because she talks about other things than her suburban childhood."

Ann turned and stared. "You mean, like my friends and I do," she said.

"Well," said Emily, "face it, Ann. A case could be made that your friends are not exactly political animals. That they care less about the world and its inequities than they care about whatever happened to . . . Shelly Moskowitz, the girl who wouldn't let you try her flute."

"Shelly *Berkowitz*," Ann said prissily, then she added, "You think my friends and I are trivial?"

"Look, just forget I said anything," said Emily. "I don't want to fight. What I want to do is remove salsa stains from the arm of this couch." She took a sponge and rubbed diligently at the couch, creating an ever-widening wet circle, but Ann could not change the subject. She was very sensitive about this matter. It worried her that she and Lisa and Meredith were so solipsistic. Maybe they were ridiculous without knowing it, just a much younger version of the claques of old widows who frequented movie matinees and restaurants that featured "early-bird specials," talking in loud, foolish voices about a wide range of foolish things. But even if it was true, was it really so terrible? Was it wrong to try to find a safe pocket in the middle of everything that felt so distinctly unsafe? Still, Ann couldn't tolerate being criticized about it. She had been born without the capacity to receive criticism. When she was eleven years old, her beloved teacher Miss Landesman had written on her report card at the end of the year, "Ann is a superb student, but my, her penmanship looks like chicken scrawl!" The remark, written in her teacher's ultra-feminine, curlicue handwriting, had deeply disturbed Ann. She had gone out and bought herself a book called *Five Steps to Better Handwriting* and had spent her summer tracing capital *W*'s and *F*'s by flashlight in bed at night, but throughout her life she had still always felt slightly ashamed of the way the ink formed itself when it came out of her pen.

"I may not be political," Ann said in a quavering voice, "but I care about important things. I mean, I *agonize*. I agonize over what's going to happen to the world, and I agonize about you. What do I have to do to prove it?"

"You don't have to do anything," Emily said calmly. "I know exactly who you are, and I'm not complaining. I don't want you to turn into Naomi. That's not what I'm saying at all. Naomi is a bore."

en

hroughout college and her early twenties, Lisa had been designated the abortion chaperone among her circle of friends. She accompanied fearful women to doctors' offices and clinics, holding their hands and steadying them as they woozily went home. At night, she made them her signature potato-leek soup, and rented funny videos for them to watch. The men who had impregnated these women were often out of the picture when it came time for an abortion, and even if they were still around, the pregnant women always seemed to prefer the comfort of their friends over the dumbstruck worry of the impregnating men. It had never occurred to Lisa that she might one day find herself accidentally pregnant. She had always thought that perhaps she was infertile, since she was one of the few women she knew who hadn't ever slipped up and missed a period. She was always so responsible, so cautious, preparing another round of contraception the way she used to prepare experiments in chemistry class. *Hypothesis: A teaspoonful of nonoxynol-9, applied carefully to the inside of a diaphragm's dome, will prevent the unwanted creation of life nine months later.* Lisa actually imagined that her seriousness of purpose conferred on her a kind of immunity, keeping her free from the problems of her more madcap friends.

She had once read of a syndrome in a psychiatric textbook called scrupulosity, in which the patient, invariably a young woman, feels a compulsion to be actively *good* at all times, to be busily engaged in the act of goodness. It was speculated that many female saints in history had suffered from scrupulosity, and that the auras around them were only the feverish light of their own manic do-gooding activity. So maybe this applied to Lisa; maybe she wasn't really so special and saintly. Maybe she was just like everyone else, her body buzzing and blooming with its own big plans.

One morning Lisa woke up with a stirring in her stomach. Eric was already at the office, performing a chemical peel on a minor soap opera actress. When Lisa sat up in bed she suddenly began to heave, and she ran gasping to the bathroom. She had vomited very few times in her life; the last time had been during college, after eating the cafeteria's Cape Cod Seafood Jumble. That incident had been easily explained; she had even thought that one of the scallops had looked gray-green and dubious. But what was this?

She washed her face and sat shakily on the closed toilet, doing a few calculations in her head: Yes, her period was late, but that occasionally happened to her during times of stress, and she and Eric had been arguing a lot lately, so she had thought this qualified as a time of stress. All she wanted now was to be with Meredith and Ann. She wanted them to be there when she found out whether she was pregnant or not. Somehow, she realized guiltily, she didn't particularly want Eric around at the moment of reckoning. When it came right down to it, she was just as faithless as those women she had taken for abortions, wanting only her friends there when she found out what her future would be.

The sheet of instructions was folded as tightly as origami. Meredith fumbled to open it. "It says here that if it stays white," she said, "you're not pregnant. But if it turns pink, you are. You know, in the future, when they have the technology, they should make it turn pink if it's a girl, and blue if it's a boy."

"Brilliant, Meredith," said Ann. "You should register that idea with the patent office."

"Will you two stop it?" said Lisa. "I feel sick enough already."

She sat on the edge of the couch, drumming on the coffee table. They had poured a little test tube of her urine a few minutes earlier, and now all they had to do was wait. The little well with the urine in it remained a safe and unchanging white. It seemed unlikely that it could suddenly turn bright pink. In fact, it seemed impossible. Lisa stopped drumming and sat back against the pillow.

"I have taken so many of these tests over the years," Meredith said, "and they're all different. It's like every company tries to do it in some cute way; the little circle thing turns pink, or a blue line appears, or you see the words 'Hey Girl, You're Knocked Up!' Why can't they all do it the same way? Why do they need a gimmick?"

"I refuse to believe this is actually going to turn pink," Ann said. "I mean, just look at it. It's white, right? It's like a sheet of paper. You're going to be fine, Lisa. You're too careful to get yourself pregnant. You're too scientific. Things like this don't happen to you."

"Oh, do you really think it'll be okay?" Lisa asked in a tiny voice.

Her voice was as pathetic as Meredith's had been, when she'd begged Lisa to give her an HIV test. Lisa had been sure that Meredith would test negative, and of course she had, and the subject of AIDS had been dropped. But now she knew the panic and the sense of doom that Meredith must have felt as she waited for a few cells to react to some chemicals and dye. The answer was only minutes away in this cheap little test. No matter how good Lisa had always been, no matter how exacting, how benevolent, no matter how many old people she had comforted, or saved, or even eased into death, she could still be pregnant. She wasn't special.

They waited. Nobody blinked. They watched the little well, in which Lisa's warm urine cooled and distilled. This was even getting a little boring. Ann stretched, silently yawned like a cat. They all began to relax. And then, suddenly, the circle popped into color. It didn't even darken slowly, like a sky at sunset going from white to pink to dark pink to red, but simply changed, switching from white to red. Lisa was reminded of the dot in the middle of an Indian woman's forehead. "Oh God, what am I going to do?" she asked in that same pathetic voice. "I'm too young to have a baby."

"Excuse me, Lisa," said Meredith, "but you happen to be twenty-nine. In some cultures that's menopause."

"If you were an Eskimo," said Ann, "you'd be put out on an iceberg."

"So how did it happen?" Meredith asked. "Were you careless?"

"No!" Lisa insisted. "My diaphragm always worked perfectly. Eric came up with a nickname for it: Princess Di. Oh, he will positively freak," said Lisa. "This is all he needs. He's desperately trying to build up his practice, and he's wiped out when he gets home at night. And besides, where would the baby sleep, in the rowing machine? And my job, what about my job? Oh God, I'm twenty-nine years old, and I'm supposed to know what to do. I make huge decisions every day—whether or not to pull the plug on people. But I just do not want to deal with having a baby."

"So don't," said Meredith. "Have an abortion. Join the club."

"I don't know if I could go through with it," said Lisa. "It's not like I've gotten pregnant with some stranger's baby. It's not like I'm some teenager in one of those books we used to read."

"Jenny's Decision," said Ann. "That was the best of them. Jenny Robertson was head cheerleader at Grovedale High and her boyfriend Keith was captain of the football team, and they both had a really promising future, except they threw it away because she let him put it in her underneath the bleachers of the football stadium one night when he got drunk after a big game. They got married and had the baby, and had to move in with her parents, and it was so terrible she just cried and cried. At the end of the book she thinks about how someday maybe their daughter will get to go to college and have the life she couldn't have."

"I'm *married,*" said Lisa. "This is Eric's baby. How

could I get rid of a baby that belongs to us? If I had an abortion and then had another baby with him a few years from now, I would always wonder what that other one had been like. The one we killed."

"Killed? God, Lisa, you sound like some rabid Right to Lifer," said Ann.

"You know I'm totally pro-choice," said Lisa. "But right now I can't bear to think about having an abortion."

"It's really not so bad," said Meredith. "You bleed like a pig, but that's the worst of it."

"But didn't you ever feel sad about it?" Lisa asked her. "You know, later?"

"Sad? Of course," said Meredith. "I'm not hard-hearted, Lisa. I do have maternal instincts, contrary to popular belief. I cried a lot a week later. I thought about what the baby would have been like. I tried to picture it. I even came up with names."

"Names?" said Ann. "What names?"

"Dylan, if it was a boy, Anastasia, if it was a girl," said Meredith. "But that was just to drive myself crazy, you know, like when you have a toothache and you keep poking at the tooth anyway, even though you know it will hurt. It's as though, for some reason, I wanted to push myself to the brink, to force myself to imagine this baby I would never meet."

"That is the saddest thing I ever heard," said Ann. *"The baby you would never meet."*

"Are you both trying to torture me?" Lisa asked. "Is that it? I don't want to hear emotional things right now. I just want to make a decision, the way I make any other decision. Logically. Pros and cons. But you're making this so . . . female."

"That's why you asked us to come over, isn't it?" asked

136

Ann. "I mean, you didn't even call Eric yet, did you?"

"I guess I should," said Lisa, but she didn't get up. Instead, she reached forward and picked up the pregnancy test. The pink dot still shone in the well, although a little less brightly now, as if there was a battery inside that charged the thing in the initial moments of emotion and shock, and then burned itself out as you got used to the idea.

Tuesday night was Lamaze night. Eric and Lisa would meet in the basement of the hospital a few minutes before the class began and share a quick sandwich. It was oddly like a date, sitting beside Eric on a bench in the grim hospital hallway, eating a sodden egg salad on white that had come out of a vending machine, and drinking diet Pepsi, even though Lisa worried about the effects on a fetus of the mysterious chemical compound jauntily named NutraSweet. Lisa was one of those jumbo pregnant women, the kind you could locate a mile away, the kind who spread out not only in front but also on the sides, so that her whole body in a pastel springtime maternity dress gave her the appearance of one of those pirouetting female hippos in *Fantasia*.

Pregnancy had seemed to take an extreme toll on Eric, who looked gaunt and exhausted much of the time. He was deeply worried about money, and had invited an investment specialist to the apartment one night to discuss zero coupon bonds. The man, whose name was Len Dubitsky, brought a few pie charts with him, one of which included the cost of college in eighteen years. The sum was so high, so unimaginable, that Eric began to sweat. Within minutes, his entire face was streaming. "Maybe the baby won't want to go to college," Lisa had said, trying to joke him out of his panic. "Maybe he'll want to become an air-traffic controller, or a disc jockey, or an Amway salesman."

"Hey," said Len Dubitsky, growing a little worried, "college is very important."

Now the baby was about to appear, and they had no investments, no stock portfolio, no stash of money for education or orthodontia or even those natural wooden toys carved in Vermont. They had no room to put a baby in their apartment, and yet they could not afford to move. Ann came over one afternoon and looked around, saying, "Think room dividers. Think Japanese screens. Use your imagination," but it did no good, because Lisa had no imagination; it was just another enzyme she had been born without. She was so literal, she could not conjure up anything that wasn't right in front of her. Although she had delivered many babies during her OB rotation, had listened to their unearthly first squalls and given them Apgar scores, she could not even begin to imagine the baby inside her.

Childbirth class was taught by a young woman named Melanie, who showed films of deliveries from many lands, including a stop in Indonesia, where, to the accompaniment of a lilting bamboo flute, women squatted alone in fields and let their babies simply slither out into the tall grass. Lisa and Eric, the two doctors in the room, turned to each other, smirking in the dark, as if to say, yeah, right. Tell me about it. When Lisa's water broke one afternoon the following month, there was no bamboo flute, no field of waving grass, no comfort to be had anywhere. They had brought along a cassette tape deck to the hospital in her overnight bag, and had packed a couple of her favorite old Joni Mitchell tapes, but she couldn't bear to listen to anything. When Eric pulled out a bottle of almond-scented body oil and tried to massage her back, as Melanie had suggested, Lisa pushed him away. She did not want to be touched. She wanted to die. If someone had left a loaded gun here on the nightstand of this room beside the fetal monitor and the forceps, she would have seriously considered putting it to her head. She tossed and heaved and panted, and she thought how terrible it was that women had to go through this, and she felt bonded to womankind in some new way, and even had a fantasy of joining NOW after the baby was born, of going to meetings, writing to Congressmen.

But when the baby was finally out, the room grew extraordinarily quiet, and Lisa completely forgot that she had become a momentary feminist, and that she had vowed never to do this again. It was like Lois Lane finally finding out who Superman really is, then immediately having a spell cast over her so she forgets everything. Lisa lay in the little birthing room, with its Laura Ashley wallpaper that had been dashed like an action painting with her own blood, while Eric wept silent, new-father tears and while her doctor, a female friend from medical school, stitched up the episiotomy and Lisa called first her parents, then Meredith, then Ann.

"I do not believe this," Meredith said that night when she and Ann and Lisa were all sitting in the hospital room, and Joshua was pathetically attempting to nurse but kept falling asleep. "You're a mother. This is your *baby*. One of us has actually had a baby."

"You're going to start saying things like 'Did you floss?'" said Ann, or "'Did you say thank you to Aunt Norma?'"

"There is no Aunt Norma," said Lisa. "And you're both just being melodramatic, the way you were when I got married. I'm not going to change."

But they knew that she already had. This bigger, older, more capable version of herself was wearing a pale yellow hospital gown and trying to get a seven-pound baby boy to stay awake long enough to siphon a little milk from her breasts. She was distracted and nervous, and all she could think about was Joshua. Motherhood, apparently, was not a place you could take your friends.

At home, Lisa's parents had provided her with a baby nurse for the first two weeks, and this too turned out to be a horrible, though necessary, experience. The nurse, whose name was Dunya, and who had a melodic, folk-tale accent of the Steppes but the strident, tyrannical demeanor of a gym teacher, brought Joshua into the bedroom for feedings at all hours of the night. Lisa would wake up and see this small woman standing over the bed, clutching the swaddled package that was Joshua. Eric barely woke, but just grunted and rolled over, while Dunya helped Lisa get the baby into position. "Here, you do it like this, Miss," Dunya said, hoisting Lisa's breast up as though it were a door knocker. Nursing wasn't easy, and it hurt a good deal at first, and Lisa found herself bursting into tears once at three A.M., while Dunya loomed over the bed and the baby couldn't seem to get any milk.

"I don't know what the problem is," Lisa said.

Dunya gave her a hard look. "Problem is," she said, "your boobs are flat and your milk is coming in slow."

It wasn't meant as an insult, but it made Lisa sob. She

felt so far away from the world of her friends, and from her own youth. Meredith and Ann didn't understand. Ann even said to Lisa on the phone, "Look, I know you're crazed, but why don't you come to the movies with me? They're showing a Barbara Stanwyck double bill at Theatre 80. Maybe it would help you escape a little." Ann just didn't get it. No one did. Lisa felt like the girl who was buried alive, and who shouted and shouted but no one heard her.

During the night, Dunya roamed the apartment, bringing in the baby, changing diapers, settling the baby back to sleep, and during the day she slept on the living-room couch, so that Lisa and Eric had to tiptoe around her and whisper. If they accidentally woke Dunya up, she would be very unpleasant and would complain for hours. Sometimes when Joshua was sleeping during the late afternoon, Dunya would rise and watch TV. She favored the home shopping network, where costume jewelry and picture frames filled the screen, and a giddy hostess fielded phone calls. Joshua slept through this parade of consumerism, his bassinet a mere two feet from the TV.

When Dunya left after the second week, Lisa and Eric were both relieved and terrified. They were excited at the prospect of using their living room again, but they were also frightened of being in charge of this tiny baby. "I don't think we should be trusted," Lisa whispered to Eric one night at three in the morning, when the baby was crying and could not be consoled. "We don't know what we're doing. We could drop him. We could drown him."

It was like medical school all over again, where you were so tired, so frazzled and bug-eyed that you were afraid you might make a mistake and kill somebody. Only now, the person you might kill was your baby. Lisa fixated on crib death, and peered over the edge of the bassinet again and again, looking for that rise and fall of the baby's breathing. The baby breathed; the motor had been set in motion, and it had no reason to stop. Sometimes, Lisa stared at the baby and became convinced he had a dreadful disease. This, too, was just like medical school, during which every student came down with an array of invisible rashes, bumps, and tumors. She sat beside Joshua's bassinet, weeping and flipping through a pediatrics textbook, until Eric yanked her away.

The apartment quickly became a warehouse of baby things. There was so much equipment required just to keep this tiny thing happy. What did they do in the old days, before the invention of battery-operated swings and electric bottle-warmers and mobiles that played an endless cycle of "It's a Small World, After All"? They lived in simple log cabins and ate hardtack, whatever that was, and the children played with a rag that had been tied into the approximate shape of a doll, and no one ever complained.

Dunya had said that Joshua was an easy baby. "He's a good boy," she had said. "If he changes sudden-like, it will be the colic. Mark my words." In the beginning, Joshua appeared to be calm, nursing and sleeping and making those faces that prompted the "smiling versus gas" debate. But at age three weeks, it was apparent that gas fueled this child. Joshua suddenly became a screaming hellcat, a colicky baby who could not be satisfied. His skinny chicken body exploded into farts, his face turning red, his arms flailing. Nothing could calm him down, and all the "tips" for colic in that book that told you how to survive your baby's first months were useless. *Take your colicky baby out for a car ride,* urged the book, but of course they had no car. *Put your colicky baby on the top of the washing machine; the vibrations will soothe him,* said the book, but they had no washing machine, and the laundry room in their building was a creepy, damp, fluorescent place that closed at 9 P.M. ever since a young female tenant had been fondled by one of the handymen during the spin cycle.

Joshua screamed and exploded into gas day and night. During that time, Lisa and Eric rarely touched each other. Sex hurt terribly, and after a while, they gave up and simply turned on the TV to watch Letterman. Life with Joshua had made their household grim and sad, as though there had been a death there, not a birth. Joshua was miserable; they all were.

And then, one weekend, when the baby was exactly three months old, he suddenly looked up at them with a new, puzzled expression, as though surprised to find them there. Then he murmured. He laughed, he began to swat at things. He became theirs. All was not lost.

When the weather cleared, Lisa took Joshua outside more often, joining the ranks of new mothers marching behind the bonnets of big carriages or behind smaller, sleeker strollers, marching, marching, ever marching, not because they enjoyed it, but because they had a baby on their hands and nowhere to go. They were like the living dead, these mothers, their legs carrying them to the bright, wide-aisled haven of the supermarket one more time, even though they had just been there that very morning. It didn't matter; they could always find something to buy. Sometimes they left with nothing more than a jar of cornichons in hand. Lisa had returned to work on a reduced schedule. When she was at the hospital, a baby-sitter named Mrs. Griffith came to watch Joshua. She was a warm, pleasant woman, but still Lisa was nervous leaving the baby with anyone she didn't know well.

"It's perfectly safe," Ann insisted, when Lisa admitted her fears.

"I just hate that Joshua has this whole life with Mrs. Griffith that I know nothing about," said Lisa. "And it's not like he can tell me what they did all day."

"That's true," said Meredith. "Remember Ellen and Mark Goldstein? I heard that their nanny had been taking the baby to Santería meetings. I think they found out because there was chicken blood on the baby's Snugli—"

"That sounds totally apocryphal," said Lisa. She had to trust the sitter; she had to assume everything was fine. And when she was with the baby, it *was* fine. Sometimes on weekends, she tried to get Ann to go for walks with her and the baby. Ann enjoyed the novelty of wheeling a stroller, and had a fantasy that Joshua would call her Aunt Ann when he got older, and that she would be his cool aunt, the one who took him to see experimental plays at rickety theaters in the East Village, and helped him cope with his own sexual confusion when his hormones kicked in.

One Saturday, Lisa and Ann wheeled Joshua to Zabar's. They bought a chocolate babka which weighed almost as much as Joshua had at birth, and then they just strolled around the store gazing with desire at all the appealing things: glazed apricots and orange slices that shone like polished glass, artichoke hearts nestled snugly inside a cylinder that was like an aquarium. There were so many unencumbered Upper West Side couples here, recently out of bed, still sleepy as bears, the man buying herring, the woman scooping mocha java into a paper bag. Lisa and Ann found themselves at the appetizing counter, where Lisa decided to buy some Westphalian ham.

"Careful, Lisa," said Ann, as they watched the man behind the counter place the big pink ham on the slicer. "Mama Cass choked to death on a ham sandwich."

"God, you are so morbid," said Lisa.

"If Mama Cass had only shared her sandwich with Karen Carpenter, they'd both be alive today," said Ann.

Suddenly a voice said, "Excuse me, how much is the gravlax?" Ann and Lisa turned in unison and saw Meredith standing a few feet away. At that moment she saw them, too. "Oh my God, hi!" she said, and Lisa wasn't sure, but it seemed as though Meredith was embarrassed, as though they had caught her in the act of doing something illegal, like shoplifting, stuffing glazed apricots up her blouse. Lisa noticed that Meredith's shopping cart was piled high with goods.

"What are you doing," asked Lisa, "stocking a bomb shelter?"

"Actually," said Meredith, "I just needed a few things."

"Oh, sure," said Ann, walking over and peering down into Meredith's cart. "Some of the four basic food groups. Like . . ." She scrabbled around in the cart and pulled out a tin. ". . . like mesquite-smoke oysters. A real staple. No home should be without."

"So I'm having a few people over," said Meredith. "Is it a felony?"

"You don't have to get defensive," said Lisa.

"It's really not a big party," Meredith went on. "It's hardly a party at all."

"More of a get-together," said Ann. "A singalong, maybe. Kind of a Mitch Miller thing."

"Look," Meredith said with false brightness, "do you both want to come? Because it would be fine, really."

"No, but thanks, Meredith," Lisa said. "Let's just drop it, okay?"

"The only reason I didn't invite you," Meredith said, "is because it's mostly TV people."

"I see," said Ann. "Just a couple of cameramen, right? And maybe a gaffer. What *is* a gaffer, anyway?"

"Look," said Meredith, "there *are* going to be some TV personalities there. You know, the Wok Lady, and those husband and wife movie critics. If you guys want to come, that would be great. But I'd have to ask you to come alone—I mean without Eric and Emily. No offense or anything, but I just don't have the room."

"Can we please just forget it?" asked Ann. "This is getting embarrassing."

"Anyway," said Lisa, "we've got to go. I have to feed Joshua."

Ann reached into Meredith's cart and retrieved the oysters, saying, "Maybe he'd like one of these."

Were they that embarrassing? Lisa wondered as she wheeled the baby home through the park, tearing off ragged pieces of her half of the chocolate babka. She wanted to cry; she wanted to sit right down on a bench in the park, among this fleet of other recent mothers and veteran nannies. She would sit and sob, and one of the other women would offer her a tissue, because that's the way women were. But she just kept walking, picking up her pace so sharply that the baby turned to look at her in surprise. Poor Joshua, she thought. He has such an embarrassing mother. And an embarrassing father, too. A set of parents who are too unsophisticated to mingle with husband-and-wife movie critics, or a woman who stir-fries for a living.

She felt a swell of love for Eric as she pushed the stroller and peered down at the top of their baby's head. The bones in Joshua's skull had not fully joined together yet; the head still had that slightly indented, fragile melon look. This head had been created by Lisa and Eric; she wanted to rush home to the other creator of the head. That was where she belonged, surrounded by the men in her life. She realized, as she pushed the stroller home at a frantic pace, its net baby bag swinging wildly, that she probably looked a little insane right now, like one of those mothers in the city who is fueled by an urgency only she can understand.

At home, Eric was stepping out of the shower. He had worked all morning, and now was done for the day. Springsteen was on, singing a plaintive, desperate song about a teenaged couple having a baby and ruining their lives forever. Lisa left the stroller in the front hall and unstrapped Joshua, carrying him over her shoulder into the bathroom. Eric was wearing only a towel around his waist, and the bathroom was still warm and wet, and fragrant from the tropical scent of creme rinse. Lisa sat on the toilet, and the baby played with the toothbrushes in their holder.

"So," Lisa said in a trembling voice, "Meredith is having a dinner party and she didn't invite us!" And then she began to cry.

"Hold on. What's this about?" Eric said. "You're crying because we didn't get invited to Meredith's party?"

"Yes," said Lisa.

"Well, who cares about some snotty party?" said Eric. "It's not worth crying over." But Lisa began to sob harder now, and Joshua looked at her with what she could have sworn was compassion.

"Oh, come on now," said Eric. "Why is it upsetting you so much? You don't like that kind of party, anyway."

"I know," said Lisa, wiping her eyes. "I'm always afraid someone's going to pull out a map and say 'Find Bosnia.' But I hate the idea that she thinks we're so embarrassing. *Are* we embarrassing? Is that it? I know that our life is completely boring to someone like Meredith. I know that she has no interest in hearing about cracked nipples, or how to choose a car seat for the baby. But I'm sorry, that's what's in my head. Does it make us that unpresentable? Does she really believe we would ruin her dinner party?"

"Oh Lisa," said Eric, "Meredith is such a snob. I've told you and I've told you. It was only a matter of time before something like this happened. And Ann is such a nut, with all her 'I Am Woman' lesbian ranting. Look, you have to face the fact that you and your friends have changed. This happens. I know it's hard, but finally you have to say: *Fuck them.* They don't deserve you. Now come here."

He tilted her head up to his, and they kissed, while the baby in her lap watched. The wet warmth of Eric's body, and the rough threads of his towel, turned the moment suddenly sexual, rather than simply consoling. After they put the baby down in his crib, Lisa went into the bedroom where Eric was waiting. He hadn't put on his clothes, and his hair was still wet. He closed his magazine and looked up at her, smiling. He was pleased because they had arrived at this moment without words, without an argument, and without that sure passion-killer, the baby, yowling in the next room. The infant monitor, their constant companion, shone its steady red light on the nightstand. Lisa moved herself on top of Eric, who already had an erection beneath the blanket. He looked so much better right now than in his photograph on the subway, his mouth open, his hair still a wet tangle that made him look vaguely Italian and threatening.

"Oh, God, Lisa," said Eric in a deep voice that she hadn't heard in a long time.

"Oh, Eric," she said in return, and all of a sudden her breasts began to spurt milk, two weak, thin streams, as harmless as old-fashioned water pistols. Milk drizzled down on Eric's chest and neck. He pulled away, more in surprise than anything else.

"Jesus, Lisa," he said, trying to laugh and be a good sport. She dabbed at him with a tissue, and they shut off the light and resumed making love, but it wasn't the same. Lisa was no longer a lover; she had been turned into a milk cow, a sad, pent-up old Bossy whose life, from birth to death, was all about function, and nothing else. Once you had a baby, was there nowhere you could go to forget about that baby for a little while? Wasn't there a small fraction of the day or night when you didn't have to smell like piss and milk and the cloying, petroleum scent of A&D ointment? Apparently, the answer was no.

They slept for a while after sex, their arms thrown about each other as in the old days, but at midnight, Lisa could hear Joshua begin to cry over the baby monitor. Lisa swung her legs over the side of the bed and pulled on her robe. She was sitting out in the living room nursing, flipping around the TV dial and finally settling on one of those full-length infomercials, in which faded TV actors gave impassioned testimony about hair thickeners or steak knives, when Eric came out of the bedroom in his robe and sat beside her.

"Go back to bed," she whispered. "You don't need to be up."

"No," he said. "I couldn't sleep."

He put his arm around her, and she thought how she and Eric ought to do their own infomercial about the wonders of marriage and parenthood. The apartment was cramped, but right now in the darkness, all the offending objects were distorted into the shapes of benign large animals in a child's storybook. The baby made a sound that came out, oddly, like the word *lip,* and Lisa and Eric both chuckled together. It was a good thing that most parents had partners, Lisa thought; if you didn't, then who else could you find to laugh at the same corny details about your kid? Who else would care that their baby had made a noise that sounded like the word *lip?* No one, she knew. No one would care. But the "lip" anecdote was something that Lisa and Eric could joke about forever.

"So," said Eric, "I got a call today from Uncle Joel. He says we should come down to Wilmington some weekend."

Lisa thought about Eric's uncles, with their identical, odd-shaped noses and their thriving dermatological practice. She couldn't imagine wanting to spend the weekend with either of them. "Wilmington isn't on my top-ten list," Lisa said.

"Actually," said Eric, "he wondered if *I* wanted to come down. To help out in his practice for a few weeks."

"But you have a job here," said Lisa.

"I could get an emergency leave," Eric said. "Here's

the thing: He and Uncle Mort are thinking of asking me to join their practice. This would be a trial run."

"But they live in Delaware."

"So we'd move," said Eric. "You could get a job in a second. Everybody loves you, and women doctors are very popular."

"I can't move," said Lisa.

"Why not?"

"Well, for one thing, my friends," she said.

"Oh, your friends," said Eric. "That's right, your best friend Meredith Grey, who loves you so much she can't even invite you to her dinner party."

"Well, I know I said that," began Lisa, and her urge was to somehow come to Meredith's defense, but Eric interrupted her.

"Look, I'm jumping the gun," he said. "They haven't offered me a job yet. Just this eight-week trial run."

"So what did you say?" Lisa asked.

"I said yes."

He had said yes; he was going to simply walk out on Lisa and the baby for eight weeks, then breeze back in to pack them up and move them down to Delaware into the bosom of his family, which showed Zinn family movies on the first Tuesday night of every month. Delaware, home of the Water Gap. Delaware, that tiny wedged-in "De." on the map; Delaware, the place where Eric had grown up and had longed to leave, and where his parents now lived their quiet Delaware lifestyle, and where Eric wanted to bring her, to turn her into a Delaware woman, and Joshua into a Delaware boy. "You said *yes*?" said Lisa. "Without even consulting me? You're going to take off for eight weeks and leave us stranded?"

"Oh, you'll be fine," said Eric.

At that moment, the baby lifted his head from her breast, and she rubbed his back until a burp came forth, then quickly switched him to the other side, as though flipping an LP. "You can't wait to get out of here, Eric," she said. "Admit it."

"Admit what? That things have gotten out of hand? That we don't have an inch of space? That I can't take a leak in the night without tripping over a goddamn . . . Smurf? That we pay huge sums of money to live like refugees?"

"For your information, refugees do not have a door-man," said Lisa.

"You want me to admit that our life has turned to shit?" Eric said. "Fine, I admit it. Is that so terrible? Lisa, come on, I love you so much, but of course I think about getting away. About having a house, and a lawn. And having a job where I don't have to plaster my face across fucking subway trains to make a living."

"I can't believe what I'm hearing," Lisa said. "We were going to have this fabulous life, right? You wanted to do big, important things. It was going to be . . . what did you call it once? A *voyage*. And now you spend your days discussing cellulite and money, and all you care about is yourself. Frankly, I don't give a fuck about Wilmington."

"Well, I do," said Eric.

"Then just go there," Lisa said. "Tonight."

"Fine," said Eric. The baby unlatched himself and arched his back. Lisa thrust him into Eric's lap and stood up, walking over to the rubber tree. With both hands, she uprooted the tree from its pot, dirt and all.

"Lisa. Lisa. What are you doing?" Eric asked.

"What does it look like?" she said. The whole clump came up with surprising ease, like a tooth that was ready to fall out. Dirt rained down to the carpet. The tree was lightweight. She held it in one hand, and with the other hand she pulled off a few remaining leaves, until there was only one left. Eric just stared at her, mystified, as she plucked out this final leaf in shaky, crazed triumph. "There," she said. "The last leaf."

leven

She woke them both from their sleep, which was unusual for Lisa, whose sense of consideration was so Girl-Scout strong that she never liked to call anyone before eleven-fifteen in the morning, just in case. For other people, eleven A.M. would have been a generous, safe bet, but Lisa tacked on those fifteen extra minutes out of a sense of courtesy, or a distorted sense of the rest of the world, those people without infants or hospital residencies. She imagined the rest of the world as having no cares, no responsibilities. For all she knew, most people slept with an eye mask on until noon, then woke up, donned a frilly bed jacket and ate bonbons.

But Meredith was up at eight, doing her Royal Canadian calisthenics in front of the TV, which played around-the-world highlights on CNN. She could stretch and shape her body, while at the same time strengthening and focusing her mind. She was in the middle of a set of abdominals when the telephone rang and it was Lisa. The voice frightened her. It sounded like Lisa through a thick layer of cheesecloth, like someone posing as Lisa.

"Eric and I broke up," Lisa said. "Our marriage is over." When Meredith, who was shocked, said she would be right over, Lisa didn't object.

Going through the park in the taxi, Meredith realized how much she enjoyed coming to Lisa's aid. It was novel, an unusual thing to do, rushing in a taxi with a bag of seedless clementines to save her best friend, when she herself was accustomed to always being saved. When she got to the apartment, though, she was disappointed to find that Ann had been summoned too, and had somehow managed to arrive before Meredith. "Oh, hi," Meredith said dully, and Ann nodded. Lisa's apartment was a wreck, with all its bulky baby furniture, and that big plant lying on its side across the rug, dirt spilled all around it. Lisa herself looked different, out of control, like someone who would live in an apartment like this one.

"Lisa," Meredith said when she walked in, "your marriage is not over."

"Yes it is," said Lisa. "See for yourself." And she pointed to the rubber tree. Ann and Meredith looked at each other, puzzled.

"You'll work it out," said Ann. "You'll go into couples therapy. They have these new techniques now. You hit each other with giant rubber mallets."

"Eric couldn't wait to get away," said Lisa. "He just packed his bags and left. And you know what? I say good riddance."

"Yeah," echoed Ann. "Good riddance."

Lisa and Meredith studied her with surprise. "You agree with me?" Lisa asked.

"Well," said Ann, "you're my friend, and he's making you miserable."

156

"But you think I'm better off?" asked Lisa.

"I wouldn't want to say better off," Ann began, and her voice faded out.

"No, really," said Lisa. "I want to know what you think. Both of you. About Eric."

"Lisa, he's your husband," said Meredith.

"So?" said Lisa. "We have no relationship. We almost never have sex. My diaphragm hardly ever leaves its little pink clamshell. I should have it bronzed. That's what marriage is like."

"Now, not all marriages," said Meredith.

"Just the ones where the people aren't right for each other," said Ann.

"You don't think we're right for each other?" Lisa asked. There was an uneasy silence, and no one would answer her. Meredith wouldn't even meet her gaze. It was a terrible moment, one they had been studiously avoiding for a couple of years. "What do *you* think, Meredith?" Lisa persisted. "Go ahead, it won't hurt me. I mean, it's important that I know these things."

"Well," Meredith began, "when you first met Eric and told us you were in love with him, I guess I was surprised, because he was so . . . uptight."

"Go on," Lisa said.

Meredith felt herself relax a little. This wasn't so terrible, after all. Lisa seemed to really want to know the truth; she seemed to want to see things through Meredith's eyes, as though Meredith possessed the larger, clearer point of view. Meredith almost felt flattered, and this gave her a measure of bravery. "So I tried to be happy because you were happy," she continued. "But now that you're *un*happy, I guess I don't have to be happy anymore."

Ann seemed to get into the spirit of this, and she added, "My sentiments exactly."

"You see," said Meredith, beginning to free-associate now, "it's like this with so many couples. The woman is the salt of the earth, and the man is the slug."

"Doesn't salt kill slugs?" mused Ann.

"Eric is very smart and all," said Meredith, "and I'm sure he's a perfectly good dermatologist. But I never know what to say to him. Whenever we're alone in a room I always wind up showing him my spider veins."

"Yeah," said Ann. "I know what you mean. All along I've just assumed he has these adorable traits that no one else can see."

She was about to tell Lisa about the first time she had met Eric, that stilted dinner party where they had the argument about *Lady Sings the Blues,* when Lisa suddenly said, "I thought you were my friends."

"We are," said Ann.

"Friends," said Lisa, "don't say this kind of thing about someone's husband."

"But Lisa, you said it first," said Meredith. "We were only echoing you. We're on *your* side."

"Are you?" asked Lisa, and it was clear that she was furious. "I don't think either of you has any idea who Eric is. You've never given him the time of day. You both think you're so superior to him, and *why?* What the hell have either of you done that's so special?"

"Now wait a minute, Lisa," said Meredith.

"I am sick of waiting," said Lisa. "I am sick of always being the patient one, the 'nice' one. All I've done my entire life is listen to your endless complaints, sitting and nodding and looking concerned, just because I'm the 'nice' one! Well, you want to know something? I am bored to death by both of you. Meredith, you have really become a joke. You're a textbook narcissist, and your problems with men are so trivial it kills me. There are real problems out there in the world, in case you hadn't noticed: people dying of AIDS by the thousands—"

"She's right, Meredith," said Ann.

"People starving to death," Lisa went on, "and you want my sympathy because you can't find a man who's perfect enough? Well, I have news for you. There is no man on earth who would satisfy you. You cannot get along with anyone. I am so sick of defending you to Ann, saying what a decent person you are underneath. I don't even think there is an underneath! Meredith, you have to be the shallowest person I have ever met."

How much more of this did Meredith have to endure? Ann seemed shocked too, but she also seemed to be experiencing a bit of *schadenfreude* at the drubbing that Meredith was taking. But then, all of a sudden, Lisa turned to Ann. "And you, Ann," she said, "you're a dyke for fifteen minutes, and suddenly you're the spokesperson for gay people everywhere. It's like you enrolled in lesbian school, and you're the valedictorian. The amazing thing is, you actually think you're oppressed. Well, I have known you longer than anyone. I have watched you take oboe lessons, and tennis lessons, and spend your summers at the Kinderwood Drama Camp for Girls. I have been with you on a Teen Tour of the Netherlands. I have seen the house you grew up in, and the big Cadillac your parents drove. I have seen your entire life. And guess what? You, Ann Lauren Rogoff, are not oppressed!"

Now she was finally finished. There was a short, stunned silence, then Ann finally found her voice and meekly said, "Look, Lisa, can we just talk about this? Can we just cool down a little, and tonight at the Lucky Wok we can sit down and discuss it like grownups."

"You don't get it, do you?" said Lisa.

"What?" said Meredith. "Get what?"

"I am done with the Lucky Wok. I never want to go there as long as I live. I am done with . . . this. This thing we have, this friendship, it's over. Do you understand?"

"Lisa!" said Ann. "Come on now."

But Lisa stood up abruptly and said, "Both of you, just get the fuck out of my life."

Half an hour later, sitting with Ann in the Lucky Wok, Meredith felt a panic attack coming on. Life without Lisa was unimaginable; it left Meredith gasping like a child who has gotten separated from her mother in the middle of a shopping mall. Lisa was gone, and she might very well never be back. Life without Lisa! Why should Meredith have to spend her life without Lisa? How would she even survive? Lisa was like a quiet force whose power you didn't comprehend until it was taken away. Like the sun. Yes, Lisa was the sun, Meredith thought, going poetic for a moment. Lisa was the sun, and now the sun had gone behind a cloud, and Meredith was left in the gray mist of the rest of her life. Friendship really was everything, Meredith thought. Maybe this was God's way of punishing Meredith for a lifetime of thinking that men were the most important beings on God's earth. Maybe God was a woman. Maybe, God forbid, God was a *lesbian*. A vengeful lesbian, like one of Ann and Emily's Queer Nation friends.

It made no sense that Meredith, who was so successful and in control, and who was now the owner of a two-bedroom co-op in what the realtor had referred to as a "white-glove building," should be reliant on someone so much less powerful than she. Lisa was always there; that was part of her charm. She was a good person, a doctorly friend who made friendship housecalls that were extremely reassuring and pleasurable, and yet Meredith had taken it all for granted. She had never expected Lisa to rise up and rebel. She had never expected anything forceful from the quiet force that was Lisa.

"I can't believe she did this to me," said Meredith as she and Ann drank their tea. "After all these years."

"Excuse me," said Ann, "but she did it to me too."

"Oh God, Ann," said Meredith, "I don't know what I'm going to do!" She put her hands to her face and began to cry.

Ann looked nervously around the room. "Meredith, please don't cry," she said. "I'm not good with crying. I don't have a shoulder to lean on. These shoulders, they're just for decoration."

"It's like she's dead!"

"She's not dead. The dead don't say 'fuck.' "

"Could you believe the way she talked to us?" asked Meredith.

"Maybe it wasn't Lisa," said Ann. "Maybe it was her evil twin, Risa."

"God knows how long she was keeping these feelings inside, just letting them *fester*," said Meredith. "It's like that rubber band ball she used to keep. We'd all give her rubber bands for it, and it got bigger and bigger, until it was the size of Greenland, and her mother threw it out."

"You know," said Ann, "if you really think about it, there's no way this friendship could have survived. Not with Eric in the picture. Love fucks up everything."

"I agree," said Meredith. "You're lucky you have Emily."

"What's that supposed to mean?" asked Ann. "I happen to love Emily."

"Well, sure, but face it, it's not the same. She's a woman."

"She is?" said Ann. "Wait a minute . . . shapely figure, wears pantyhose . . . Oh my God, you're right! I've been sleeping with a woman! Aaagh!"

"Oh, cut it out," said Meredith.

"Are you saying that the person I love isn't good enough to break up a friendship?" asked Ann.

"Look, I'm too fragile right now to fight with you," said Meredith. "I just want to go home tonight and have a good cry."

"I wish I could cry too," said Ann, "but I just feel so pissed off at her. The nerve! Here we are, her best friends in the world, the bridesmaids at her wedding, and she dumps us just like that. It's all Eric's fault. Before he came along we were totally happy. He's changed her, Meredith, don't you see? It's like *The Stepford Wives.* They all lived in this perfect little town, and their husbands had them killed and replaced by robots who made gourmet meals and cleaned the house and gave them blowjobs every night. But Katharine Ross got suspicious, and when her best friend, Paula Prentiss, started acting weird and submissive, she stabbed her in the kitchen with a steak knife, and *no blood came out,* so she knew she was a robot. But the robot went haywire, and started repeating herself." Ann began to move her arms and head like a robot, and speak in a mechanical voice. " 'I thought we were friends. Why, look at you, you need a good hot cup of coffee!' "

Meredith joined in then, moving like a robot too, saying "I thought we were friends. Why, look at you, you need a good, hot cup of coffee!" And then they both began to laugh.

"It would really piss Lisa off if she saw we were having a good time without her," said Ann. "We should become friends just to spite her."

"What are you doing next weekend?" Meredith asked. "Lisa and I were going to have a pedicure. Want to go in her place?"

"I'd love to," said Ann. "I've got these bunions, and this big callus. Hey, Paul Bunyan and Maria Callas."

"You know," said Meredith, "I always assumed Lisa kept us from killing each other, but maybe I was wrong. Maybe she kept us apart all these years. Maybe that was her secret plan."

"In a weird way," said Ann, "we're the ones who have more in common."

"We do?"

"Yes," said Ann. "For one thing, we're both very opinionated. Lisa, on the other hand, has no opinions. She's like my aunt Bev, who will watch any movie, be it *Ghostbusters*, or *The Garden of the Finzi-Continis*, and tell you it was 'cute.' "

"You could be right," said Meredith.

"And, of course," added Ann, "we're both lesbians."

"That's not funny," said Meredith.

The loss was so extreme that Meredith decided to consult a therapist. She had been in therapy once before in her life, when she was sixteen and, in a conflation of dieting mania and a recent obsession with the life of Simone Weil, had begun flirting with the idea of starving herself a little.

The therapist was a pigeon-breasted, big-mama type named Sylvia Korn-Holbein, who had, more than once, appeared in a major motion picture, playing a therapist. Her office was as soft and comfortable as she was, filled with fringed serapes from Guatemala, Mary Cassatt prints of dreamy, pink-complected women bathing their babies, and strategically placed boxes of pastel-print Kleenex. Meredith had seen the therapist for a year, during which time she lost her interest in starving herself and gained, instead, a lively interest in losing her virginity to a boy named Michael Reese.

When Michael came into the picture, Meredith barely wanted to talk to Dr. Korn-Holbein anymore. She suddenly resented the woman's gently prodding questions; they were as persistent and intrusive as her own mother's. The therapist became snippety with Meredith, as though annoyed that her young brooding patient had someone else to be intimate with, someone male. At any rate, by the time Meredith stopped therapy, she had accelerated to mutual masturbation with Michael, and had gained ten pounds from her renewed interest in food, and at her last session, Dr. Korn-Holbein gave her a slip of paper on which she had written the name of a gynecologist who would fit her with "something." The therapist seemed almost angry at Meredith. Probably, Meredith thought much later, it all came down to the fact that Meredith was about to get laid, while Dr. Korn-Holbein probably wasn't.

Now, after Lisa broke off with Meredith and Ann, Meredith decided it was time to do some serious, hardcore psychic work on herself. After looking into the matter, she decided that only classical Freudian analysis would do. She liked the idea of lying on a couch four times a week, although she was afraid it would ruin the backs of all her clothes. But a friend at the station had spoken reverently of her own analyst and had given Meredith a recommendation to see a colleague of the analyst's, a man named Leonard Pine. Meredith made an appointment, and at first she had high hopes. She even liked his name; it seemed both elegant and studious.

Leonard Pine was a thin, not inelegant man in his forties, with dark eyes and an unconstructed Italian suit. When she first lay on his couch, the sensation was strange, but after a while she began to enjoy herself. There were recessed lights in Dr. Pine's ceiling, and the only sound came from his white-noise machine, which hummed like a little unobtrusive UFO in the corner of the room. This was so different from her experience with Dr. Korn-Holbein, Meredith thought as she settled herself in for the forty-five-minute hour. Why did they call it an hour, she wondered, when it wasn't that at all? Or at least, if they called it an hour, they should put quotation marks around the word, to give it a little bit of amusing sarcasm. She remembered reading about the French psychoanalyst Lacan, who sometimes declared a session over after three minutes. *Fini!* she could imagine him saying, leaping up out of his chair, while some poor patient stared up at him from the couch, blinking in confusion like a rudely awoken sleeper.

But Dr. Pine's sessions were long and luxurious, like a good bath. He seemed to really listen, too. Outside, cars rushed by on the wet street. Meredith's appointed hour was at the end of the day, when the sun was beginning to set in that way that gave the stately buildings along Park Avenue a sad, noble valence. The street was dotted with taxis with their little yellow lights on, and with people opening umbrellas and stepping out from under awnings, while Meredith stayed unmoving in this warm, gray room with her feet up. It was simply wonderful. She liked the idea of being in treatment with Dr. Pine for years. It was not unheard of for an analysis to last a decade. Her analyst would usher her through the trauma of turning thirty, and into the rest of her life. Sure, it would be painful at times to talk of early memories that she had all but forgotten: her uncle Al, who had given one of her new breasts a covert squeeze at a family party when Meredith was eleven; the time she had come to the top of the stairs after a bad dream as a child, only to see her parents having ferocious sex on the recliner chair in the living room. But it would all be deeply cathartic, and Meredith and Dr. Pine would grow older together, and when it came time to terminate, there would be a tacit, unspoken moment of loving melancholy between them.

There would be years ahead in which to talk about sex and early-childhood stirrings, but at her first session, Meredith talked exclusively of Lisa, and of what Lisa's absence meant to her. "I don't understand how she could have done this to me," Meredith said. "It's not just that I've been such a good friend to her. It's the idea that in good conscience she could turn her back on me, and on everything we've been through, as if it never happened. Like one of those movies, where the husband breaks up with the wife suddenly, after twenty-five years of marriage. Bingo! It's over. He trades her in for something better, younger. A secretary. An aerobics instructor. Where is Lisa going to find a better friend than me? Where? You can't replace the kind of history we've had together. We've been through it all. I was there at the beginning. I even taught her how to take off a bra, using the little trick that women do."

"Um, what trick?" asked Dr. Pine.

"You know," said Meredith, "where you unhook it under your blouse and pull the whole thing off through your sleeve, so you never have to actually take off your blouse."

"Oh," said Dr. Pine. "Through the sleeve. I see."

"Who else is going to give her that?" asked Meredith. "But maybe she doesn't want that kind of friendship anymore. Maybe she just wants to be left alone. God knows, I know what that feels like. It's exactly how I felt after Alan and I broke up. Of course, it didn't last very long, because I hate being alone. I profoundly hate not having a lover."

"Oh?" said Dr. Pine. "Can you say more?"

"It makes me feel fat," said Meredith, "and homely. It makes me feel like one of those women you see sometimes in the city getting their dinners from a Korean salad bar. Just standing in their little dress from work and a pair of uncomfortable shoes, putting arugula and baby corn and no-oil dressing into a plastic container. And you just know that they're going to take the salad home and sit in front of the TV all night. It's as though they have no purpose in life, no destination, and they know it. But when I have a lover, I feel as though I have a real purpose. A reason to be. Someone to come home to, metaphorically speaking. It's like that with Lisa, too. Take our monthly dinners at the Luck Wok; I always know that they're coming up, and I look forward to them. I know what dinner will be like, sitting there with her and Ann, and talking about everything under the sun and eating hot-and-sour soup.

I miss that already! Why can't I have that? Is it so terrible that I said those things to Lisa? It's the truth, isn't it? Am I supposed to love Eric just because I love Lisa? What do you think, Dr. Pine?"

There was a long silence. Meredith turned her head and looked over at the psychiatrist, who sat in the palm of his big leather chair, his hands pressed together, his face resting on the steeple his hands made. "Meredith," he said finally. "I must tell you something."

"You think I'm a terrible friend," she said. "You agree with Lisa."

"No," said Dr. Pine, in a strained voice. "It's you. I can't treat you. I'm very sorry. I'm experiencing a rather uncomfortable, if predictable, form of counter-transference right now."

"Excuse me?" said Meredith.

"I'm very attracted to you, Meredith," he said, "and I have to admit that I haven't been listening very closely to what you've been saying. I've been trying hard, but I'm too distracted. You need someone who can listen better. I've failed you, and I'm very, very sorry. This has never happened to me before." Meredith heard rustling and saw that Dr. Pine had stood up. She sat up on the couch a little too quickly, and felt dizzy, looking up into his sad, long face.

"So that's *it*?" Meredith said.

"Well, I can give you the name of another analyst," said Dr. Pine.

But Meredith said no, she thought she'd rather go it alone. They shook hands unhappily at the door, and once again Meredith was let go.

* * *

At the Nail Nook over the weekend, Meredith and Ann sat on a raised platform while two Asian women labored over their feet. "You know," said Meredith, "I'm getting over Lisa, I really am. I didn't think it would happen, but I guess it's some kind of Elisabeth Kübler-Ross thing. The stages of grief. For a while, I was hysterical, but now I think I've begun to accept it. I've stopped thinking about Lisa all that much, and in a weird way, I even feel liberated. Do you know what I mean?"

"Actually," said Ann, "yes. It sort of amazes me how quickly we can just pick up the pieces. But I guess the moral of this is that life goes on, no matter what. It's kind of amazing."

"When I was really little," said Meredith, "we had this dachshund named Sputnik. One day he ran away, and for months I waited at the back door with a little dog yummy in my hand, calling 'Sput-nik! Sput-nik!' It was so pathetic. Of course, he never came home. But I got over it. I convinced myself that he was alive, and that he'd been taken in by a really good family somewhere, who gave him one of those air-conditioned doghouses with shag carpeting, and his own little toilet bowl he could drink from."

"Meredith," said Ann, "Lisa is not drinking from somebody's toilet. She just hates us, that's all. See, we broke the cardinal rule of friendship: Never say bad things about your best friend's husband."

"But she said them herself first," said Meredith. "We were only agreeing with her."

"It doesn't matter," said Ann. "Women stick with their men. No matter how disgusting, how depraved. I mean, if Charles Manson had an ex-wife, and you went up to her at a party and said, 'Was that Sharon Tate stuff really necessary?' she'd probably never speak to you again."

"And it would be my loss," said Meredith.

When their pedicures were done, they said good-bye and separated to go home. Meredith walked along the edge of Central Park, where men and women jogged, and bicycles zipped silently past, and where tall trees separated the west side of the city from the east. Lisa was somewhere over there on the east side, feeding her baby or taping up somebody's ankle. Meredith could picture her clearly: the sweep of her hair, the headband. *Oh, well,* she thought, peering through the park, as though she might actually get a last glimpse of Lisa in a window on the other side of the city.

Part Three

$\mathcal{T}$welve

$\mathcal{O}$ne morning, Ann was sitting at her desk trying to come up with jacket copy for another terrible first novel that Harry Corning loved, written by a young British woman who had been a heroin addict and whose father was an M.P., and whose aristocratic bearing, mixed with a jumble of funky clothes and jewelry, made her a good interview subject both here and abroad. Harry expected the book to do well, although Ann hated it. There were very few words on each page and lots of white space. Perhaps, Ann thought, that was so the reader could write comments in the margins, like a teacher grading a paper: *"Bad!" "Purple prose!" "Cliché!"* Ann was sitting and angrily trying to find a way to describe this book, when her telephone rang and it was the literary agent Evan Bright, wanting, of all things, to take her to lunch. She couldn't imagine why, and he wouldn't tell her over the phone.

At noon, Ann and Evan walked past the coffee shops where employees of Ann's rank usually ate and headed for Gepetto, where Evan held the door open for her and she finally entered the room she'd always looked at, with longing, from the outside. It was even more beautiful from inside, filled with flowers and handsome waiters and heavy, gleaming silverware. For the first twenty minutes of the meal she had no idea why she was here but the food was so splendid, so delicious and arranged on the plate so unusually, that for a while she forgot to wonder. Nobody ever took her out to a place like this! She was accustomed to the Lucky Wok and to a variety of cheapo Japanese, Greek, and Indian places that offered $4.95 lunch specials. This was way out of her range of experience. She turned to Evan, waiting. She felt that he must have gotten completely bored with powerful types, and that he wanted a refreshing breath of powerlessness across the table. Or maybe he wanted to wax nostalgic about his years at Yale with another Eli. They drank a bottle of wine and dipped heavy bricks of focaccia in olive oil, and Ann felt drunk and happy and utterly unprepared when Evan asked her to come work for him.

"What?" she said. "What do you mean, work for you? What could I possibly do for you?"

"I have an opening, Rogoff" Evan said. "An associate position. You'd be an actual literary agent, not somebody's assistant. Harry's been underusing you for years. You obviously know so much more than those pinheads there, and it's clear to me that if you don't get out now, you never will." Then Evan offered her a salary that was better than her current one by nine thousand dollars, although he warned that in a couple of years she'd have to go on straight commission, like everyone else.

Ordinarily, Ann would have said she needed a day to think about it, and then she would have rushed home to call Lisa. She would even have had Lisa paged at the hospital, and they would have met later on to talk about all the ramifications of taking a job with Evan Bright. Lisa would have helped her make a list of pros and cons. Lisa had perfected the art of the list. But now there was no Lisa to go to, only Meredith, and that wouldn't be the same. Ann stared into her wine glass. There was only a small amount left, a thin golden coin. She lifted the glass to her lips anyway, just to have something to do. Through the concavity of glass she could see Evan staring at her, waiting for her answer, his woolly dark eyebrows lifted in anticipation. God, he was weird, and everyone hated him. She'd have to be insane to work for him. The big article about him that had appeared in a magazine the year before had forever sealed his reputation as a high-rolling nutcase. He once came to work disguised in mustache and dark glasses, insisting he be let upstairs to see "the famous Mr. Bright," even though he had no appointment, just to see how tight the building security was. (Not very.) He once organized a live lobster race down the hallway of his office. He was forever throwing tantrums on the telephone to London. His wife, deeply unhappy at home with the twins, was known to occasionally show up at work, a baby under each arm, plopping them both down on his desk, saying: *Here! You take care of them for a while! You see what it's like!*

But Ann continued to enjoy Evan. It was almost perverse; surely he was irritating and bizarre and vastly vain, with his handmade shirts and his fat, expensive fountain pens that dispensed blood-red ink. But she hated her job at Eberhardt, and her job threatened to make her hate her life. There had to be something preferable, she often thought, but she always came up blank. Maybe if she were truly self-confident, like Meredith, life would open up in a wonderful way, or maybe if she were truly altruistic, like Lisa, she would feel that she had a mission. But as it was, she was a woman stuck in a job that was going nowhere, living with another woman and telling herself she was a lesbian, suffering the loss of the one friendship that had stayed true and ardent over many years. And here was Evan, beckoning with his wine glass and his Groucho eyebrows and his gleaming big teeth. So she accepted on the spot, and they spent the rest of lunch drinking heavily. When Ann returned to the office, she was as drunk and smelly and giddy as her own boss, Harry, was, whenever he returned from one of these incredible lunches.

Ann quit her job the following week and began work as a literary agent. It was shocking to finally have her own office, with a wall that went all the way up to the ceiling, and a window that overlooked Rockefeller Center. Evan was an amusing figure to see every morning, in his impeccable shirts and cufflinks. He praised Ann for every small move she made, calling her "shrewd," and "a natural," and after a while, his stroking helped her enjoy the aggressiveness of this business, the litany of threats on the telephone, the tense kinetic activity of being involved in a publishing auction. The same thin, ethereal authors whom she'd always despised at Eberhardt wandered through Evan's offices, but she no longer despised them in the same way she used to. Now, they were on her team. She couldn't resent them; she had to represent them.

The work was nerve-wracking, and at home Ann and Emily had terrible "Newlywed Game"–style fights over nothing: who was supposed to scrub the bathtub, who had left a container of yesteryear's coffee yogurt in the back of the refrigerator. Emily suggested that Ann might do well to have a weekend off, and Ann agreed. One

Friday evening, she took the train by herself out to Magatuck. She sat in the window of a three-seater and she leaned against the smeary glass and thought of all the times she had taken this trip to and from Magatuck with Lisa and Meredith. As teenagers, they actually used to ride in the city and go down to Washington Square Park to buy joints from drug dealers. If you did that now, Ann thought, you would inhale rat poison and wind up having convulsions, blood pouring out of your nose. But back in the seventies, when the world seemed open and free and relatively harmless, the three girls would roam around the city as though it were a very large paneled rec room. They went to Serendipity for lunch, sitting under the Tiffany lampshades and eating enormous ice cream sundaes, except for Meredith, who always ordered coffee, black. They went to the Burlington Mill, where they stood on a moving sidewalk that took them past exhibits about how carpeting is woven. They went to Bloomingdale's and had free makeovers, and spent the ride home trying to wipe all the color from their face before they pulled into the station in Magatuck.

Now Ann's mother was waiting in the parking lot of the train station in her sporty little red BMW that she had recently purchased. Ann's childhood had been filled with a succession of big, bulky family cars, but as soon as she became fully grown, her parents' tastes immediately changed. The week she left for Yale, they signed up for a Chinese cooking class, and lately they had been teaching themselves the art of calligraphy.

"So how's life as an agent, kiddo?" her mother asked when Ann climbed into the little car. Her mother had the radio tuned to a New Wave station.

"Oh, you know," said Ann, and during the drive to

Pleasant Meadow Court, she told anecdotes from her new job. When she ran out of things to say, she began to tell her mother all about the break-up with Lisa.

"This is too much for me to keep up with," said Adele. "First you're a lesbian, and a literary agent, and now you tell me you and Lisa aren't friends. What's next?"

They drove past Burger Man, and a discount shoe outlet, and World of Pools, and Ann was so overcome with nostalgia for her past life, the one spent with Meredith and Lisa, that she fantasized about moving back in with her parents. She wouldn't have to formally break up with Emily; she would just never return to the apartment. It was so much better here in the suburbs, at least in terms of material comfort. Here you had a choice of rooms. Here you could sleep under thick, quilted blankets, listening only to the hum of the crickets outside, and the shifting midnight gears of the refrigerator.

"Did I ever tell you," said Adele, "about the best friend I had when I was your age? Her name was Marlene Kafka."

"I think I'd remember that name," Ann said.

"Oh, she was a wonderful girl," said Adele. "We used to have the best times together. We'd go to Atlantic City for the weekend, and once we took an abstract painting class in Greenwich Village. We were extremely close. She wasn't much of a looker, Marlene Kafka. Actually, she had a face like a flounder, but she was quick with a joke."

"What does that mean, 'a face like a flounder'?" Ann asked.

"The eyes," said Adele. "They looked like they were on one side of her head. Asymmetrical. She was odd-looking, Ann. Men liked her, but frankly, not for fucking."

"Ma!" said Ann. "Watch your mouth. There are children present."

"Well, it's true," said Adele. "So sue me. Anyway, when I met your father, Marlene Kafka said she had to be honest, and that she didn't think he was interesting or cultured enough for me. So I dropped her, just like that. She offended me. She spent years trying to make it up, inviting your father and me to little get-togethers at her house. She remained single, and she was always trying to give funny little parties—wine tastings, seances, fondue nights, but we never accepted. After a while, she stopped inviting us. To this day, I don't know what happened to her. It was a beautiful friendship, but it had to end."

"This is different," Ann said, as the car bumped up into the driveway of the house. "This isn't some flounder-faced girl. This is Lisa we're talking about."

"You'll get over it," said Adele, patting Ann's knee. "You're my daughter, after all."

That was true enough, and Ann *was* getting over Lisa, but her mother clearly did not understand. Adele gave friendship a low ranking next to marriage. Women were expendable; they came and went, following their husbands to new cities, new lives, throwing themselves into the world of their children, preparing Halloween costumes and birthday parties. In her crowd, most friendships were done in couples, like a giant square dance, and Adele probably viewed Ann's attachment to Lisa as merely an outgrowth of her lesbian tendencies. The love for Julie Andrews, the clinginess to other girls; it all added up to a predictably deviant adult lifestyle. To her mother's credit, though, Adele had grown to truly like Emily. In the beginning, she had checked a book out of the library called *So Your Son or Daughter is Gay!* Lately, though, she had not only become used to the idea, but she seemed to enjoy Emily's presence. Emily was fashionable; once, Adele even took her shopping in the city, and they returned to the apartment loaded down with shopping bags, and still giggling together over something an inept saleswoman had done. Adele had truly begun to make her peace with the fact that Ann preferred women. But she would never understand about Lisa.

Over the weekend in Magatuck, Ann's parents were in constant motion. They demonstrated their calligraphic prowess for her. They cooked various Chinese dishes, glutinous with cornstarch, but still tasty. Early in the morning, they showed her how to do a yoga exercise called "Salute to the Sun." By the time Sunday afternoon came, Ann was more exhausted than ever, and ready to return to the city. On the trip back, she thought about her mother and Marlene Kafka, two girls sitting and smoking cigarettes together, in a time when no one knew that smoking sent you to an early grave. She thought about them taking an art class in the Village, standing in smocks at easels, trying desperately to re-imagine a bowl of fruit as free-floating orbs of color. Where were those sweetly terrible canvases now? Gone, discarded, like Marlene Kafka herself. Ann's mother wasn't cruel, she was merely sensible. Sometimes you just had to move on: find a new job, a new life, new friends. This was true for Ann, too: Lisa was fading fast, and in her place stood Meredith.

The following week, Ann set Meredith up on a blind date. It wasn't a date, exactly; it was a bowling party given by Emily's office at Legal Aid, held at a bowling alley in the far West 40s. What made it something of a date was the fact that Emily's handsome and available colleague Dale Sanger would be there, and Emily thought Meredith would really like him. At first, Meredith had refused to go. She had complained that she wasn't suffering from a dearth of men; she knew too many of them, in fact, and most of them were interested in her, but they were all disappointing in their own individual ways. "Come on," Ann coaxed. "You haven't been bowling since Debby Gardner's tenth birthday party at the Magatuck Lanes." To Ann's surprise, Meredith agreed to come.

So now here she was, slipping off her dusted-cocoa Manolo Blahnik pumps and trading them for a pair of bowling shoes. Sixties music was pounding through the speakers of the bowling alley: the Monkees singing "I'm a Believer," which was just the right speed for this crowd of nostalgic young do-gooding lawyers and their friends. There were bright-colored frozen drinks available at the bar, and lots of loopy, boisterous, unathletic bowling. Meredith looked across the room, and it didn't take her very long to figure out which of the men was the one Ann wanted her to meet. Dale had longish, silvery hair and a beautiful face like Montgomery Clift. He was by far the tallest, best-looking man here, and Meredith was the tallest, best-looking woman. If their long, expensive street shoes were placed side by side in the darkness of a cubbyhole, they would probably start to mate. Meredith and Dale seemed so advanced beyond this event, just slumming for the night, their hair fuller and springier than anyone else's, their bodies toned to tight perfection inside their casual clothes. They were two people who so obviously did not belong here, who were trying to be regular folks for one evening of camaraderie, two special people who belonged, right this very minute, together in bed.

Looking at him from a distance, Meredith suddenly became afraid. "I don't want to do this," she said to Ann. "I'm wearing bowling shoes! I look like a court jester. You know, you could get an infection from these shoes. A bowling fungus or something."

But suddenly it was too late to change her mind, for Emily had arrived at the bench with Dale. "Dale Sanger, this is Meredith Grey," Emily said, pointlessly, as though this god and goddess wouldn't find a way to speak to one another without her intervention.

Dale was staring at Meredith. "Meredith Grey," he said. "I love your show. I even watched you on that fundraiser last week."

"The phone drive?" said Meredith. "But I was on at four A.M."

"Well, lawyers stay up late," said Dale. "You were very charming, so I called in a pledge."

"You did?" said Meredith. "That's so sweet."

"I'm sure you get sick of people fawning over you," said Dale.

"It exhausts her," Ann said.

"Takes her days to recover," said Emily.

"But I just want to say I think you're terrific," said Dale.

"Well, thank you," said Meredith.

He stepped closer. "They sent me a mug," he said.

"For twenty-five dollars more you could have had a tote bag," said Meredith.

"Damn!" said Dale.

"My apartment is filled with tote bags," said Meredith.

"I'd like to see them sometime," Dale said.

From the sidelines, Ann and Emily watched this exchange with astonishment. "Would you look at them?" Emily whispered. "It's disgusting. Heteros in heat."

"Oh, stop," said Ann.

"I mean, you just know they're going to do it tonight," continued Emily. "Heterosexuals are so unsubtle. No nuance. He wants to fuck her, and she wants to fuck him, and that's the way it is. They probably won't be able to keep their hands off each other while they bowl. They'll be down on all fours soon right in the middle of lane six, doing it doggie-style—"

"Stop it!" said Ann again. "Come help me perfect my gutter ball." She yanked Emily away and they bowled a few sorry games, but throughout the evening Ann found herself periodically looking over at lane six to catch a glimpse of what was so clearly and enviably the progress of love.

Thirteen

*L*ike many women, Meredith tried to follow the three-date rule when it came to sex. On the first date, you made sure the other person was attractive and interesting, on the second date, you told each other a few touching and revealing personal details, so that on the third date, you could both fling headlong into bed, telling yourselves that you weren't sleeping with a stranger. Nobody seemed to know how the three-date rule had come to be, although everyone seemed aware of its existence. Men didn't have an equivalent of such a rule; if they measured chastity at all, it was in minutes, not days.

But the night that Meredith met Dale at the bowling alley, she found herself trying to compress three dates into one, so that the evening might somehow end with them making love. The flirtation had begun immediately. They stood on the varnished floor of the alley, talking for a while, and then they attempted to bowl. Dale was good at the game, although Meredith wasn't. He didn't make fun of her, but instead was sympathetic as the ball kept swerving to the left, frame after frame. At some point, he asked her if she would like a quick lesson, and she said yes. Dale stood beside her, talking about "trajectory" and "momentum," and his arm was positioned loosely around her waist, cradling her elbow. He lingered there, talking earnestly. She could feel his breath in her hair, and she imagined him kissing her neck. Finally he gave up talking altogether, and they just stood close for a moment.

"This is very strange," Meredith managed to say. "What are we doing? I don't even know you."

"I'll tell you everything," he said quickly. "I'm forty years old. Divorced. I cook one dish to impress women: chicken with pecans. Women like things with nuts, don't ask me why." He paused, looking at her. "So what about you?" he asked. "Anything I should know?"

"My real name is Guzzi," said Meredith.

"Guzzi Grey?" said Dale, confused. "What kind of a name is that?"

"Meredith Guzzi," she said. "And I'm going to be thirty in two weeks, can you believe it? I want a birthday cake with Prozac icing."

"Why?" said Dale. "Thirty is great. Wonderful things happen. I got married at thirty."

"But it didn't last, did it?" said Meredith. "I'm never getting married."

"Why would you say that?" asked Dale.

"It ruins everything," said Meredith. "I have this friend Lisa—well, she was my friend, but we don't speak anymore—and she was the first one to get married, and it wrecked her life. I mean, totally. It's very sad, what happens to people."

"This isn't sad," said Dale. "What's happening here."

"No," she said softly.

"Although," he went on, "maybe you're right. We should stop it right now, before things get too tragic." He reached out and stroked her hair, and she took in a sharp breath.

"We should get out while we can," she said, her eyes closing, chemicals kicking in.

"By the way," he said. "Love your shoes." And then they were in each other's arms.

Later that night she was waiting for him in his bed, a big dark field that bore a scent of an unfamiliar laundry detergent. The room was a little cold, but his blanket was one of those heavy goose-down quilts that pin you to the bed with the improbable weight of all those feathers. Dale's entire loft was a large, unbroken space that had no clutter to it, no hidden tumbleweeds of dust, no faint sprinkling of boric acid around the perimeter of the kitchen. A sleek black telephone rested on a curve of black marble, and the soap in the bathroom was a beige oval that sat in a dry glass dish, and not—as at some other men's apartments—in its own soup. The trappings were all more than acceptable here, and so was their owner.

Dale slipped into bed beside her and she saw that he'd quickly shaved in the bathroom—a touching gesture, probably meant to save her from the agonies of beard-burn. They began their tentative first round of touching and kissing, those pressured first minutes in which every noise is magnified: every inadvertent suction sound of kissing or syllable of arousal, and then they paused long enough to endure the obligatory HIV-status conversation:

"I've been tested," she whispered. "I'm negative."

"I've been tested too," he said.

"When?"

"Recently."

"So, how'd you do?" she said nervously.

"I passed," he said. "Although it was graded on a curve."

He wore a condom, pulling it on with the usual rueful expression, but making no sarcastic comments as he did. She was pleased to find that Dale didn't seem excessively grateful to be here with her. Whenever men seemed grateful during sex, Meredith worried that she'd inadvertently bedded a real loser. There was none of that with Dale. She could imagine a fleet of good-looking women who had been in this bed before her, and the fantasy made her feel suddenly territorial, as though she needed to try especially hard to keep him. She was pleased that she happened to be wearing expensive underwear tonight. Dale slipped them off her, and they looked ridiculous lying limp in his big hands, like the lingerie of a child stripper. He flung the black underwear into the black darkness of his room, and turned to her.

Later, Dale fell happily asleep and Meredith was still wide awake, so she got up from the bed and wandered around the apartment, doing a little research. Dale was not only a passionate, intelligent man, but all the hangers in his closet were wood! Yes, she thought, he would definitely pass the train test. She would sit with him on a ride across the entire country. Not that she would take a *train* cross-country, and even if she did, she would certainly book a sleeper. But she knew how she felt about him. Meredith was about to return to bed, satisfied, when she passed a wall of bookshelves. She saw a flash of beige and rust, and she peered upward at it, realizing that the book was *Middlemarch,* the same edition that Meredith owned. Dale liked George Eliot. Surely this was fate. He was literate, perhaps even scholarly. Maybe he would make jokes about Boswell and Dr. Johnson at cocktail parties, and she would have to pretend to understand. Now Meredith climbed the rolling ladder and plucked the book from the shelf, bringing it back to bed.

"Dale," she hissed.

"What? What?" He sat up quickly.

"You have *Middlemarch*!" she said.

"Oh. Oh, yeah, right," he said, lying back down.

"It's my favorite book," said Meredith. She paused, then decided to amend this. "Well, it would be my favorite book, if I ever finished it," she admitted. "But I haven't found the time, what with the show and everything."

"Actually, I've never read it," he said. "A woman gave it to me a long time ago, and it's just been sitting there on the shelf. I'm embarrassed to say I'm very deficient when it comes to fiction. I've sort of been living in an all-torts universe for years."

"Would you want to read it together?" she asked shyly.

"Aloud?" he said.

"Well, yes," she said. "I know some people who do little readings together. Proust, Virginia Woolf, Dante. It sort of makes it easier, because you have someone to talk about it with, you know?" She was babbling now, and felt as though she had ruined everything. "Oh God," she said, "you think this is a really retarded idea." But he simply smiled slowly at her, taking the book from her hands, and began to read.

* * *

By the time Meredith's thirtieth birthday arrived, Dale had been folded completely into her life. They knew each other's friends, they had met each other's parents, they spoke dreamily on the telephone several times a day. Who needed Lisa when she had this? In fact, it occurred to Meredith that maybe her intense friendship with Lisa had kept her from ever having an equally intense relationship with a man. At her birthday party in an ornate restaurant in Little Italy, she and Dale sat side by side, surrounded by Ann and Emily, and several people from the station, including the Wok Lady, and Hank the Handyman. Everyone was lively and well-fed, and a woman from another table had even recognized Meredith and asked her to autograph a napkin. Maybe turning thirty really wasn't so traumatic after all.

Toward the end of the evening, someone brought out a sheet cake that looked like a giant TV screen, with Meredith's likeness drawn on it in icing, and everyone ate pieces of Meredith's face and shoulders. When the waiter brought the check, Dale discreetly took it from its tray and began to study it. "Dale, no," said Meredith. "I invited everyone."

"Look, we'll all pitch in, Meredith," said Ann.

"Absolutely not," Meredith said.

"Well, I want to do something," said Ann. "At least let me leave the tip." She turned to Dale, who hesitated.

"Well, okay, if you're sure," he said. "That's very sweet of you, Ann."

Ann looked at the bill, figured it out, then put some money down. There was a pause, and then Meredith quietly began to count out Ann's tip. "Uh, Ann?" Meredith said. "Please don't take this the wrong way, but is that all you were planning to leave?"

"Of course not, Meredith," said Ann. "I also left a krugerrand under the butter dish."

"It's just that I know something about these things," Meredith went on, "and I think you should leave a bit more, if you can.

" 'If I can'?" said Ann. "What's that supposed to mean? Things are tight, but I'm not Ma Joad."

"I didn't say you were," said Meredith. "But I know you, and I thought it would be insensitive of me to presume that you actually had enough money on you to leave an appropriate tip."

"This is appropriate," said Ann. "I did the math. It's fifteen percent."

"No offense, Ann, but the going rate is twenty. I did a TV segment about tipping just last week."

"So that makes you an expert," said Ann.

"More than some people."

"You're saying that I'm not capable of leaving a tip in a restaurant?" asked Ann. "That I need some TV personality to do it for me?"

"Apparently."

"You know," said Ann, "just the other night I had dinner with Diane Sawyer. We were at a ribs joint, and she didn't even look at the tip I left." Other people had begun to listen to their conversation, but Meredith and Ann couldn't stop now. "Meredith," Ann went on, "you don't know how to get through a single evening without criticizing someone."

"This isn't criticism," insisted Meredith. "It's a firm suggestion."

"Ja, mein führer."

"Oh, fuck you," said Meredith.

"No, fuck you," said Ann.

Dale took Meredith's arm and said nervously, "I get it. This is the episode where Lucy and Ethel accidentally wear the same dress."

So they moved the argument to the ladies' room, which had rose-colored Italian tile and a countertop with a tray of various hairsprays and mouthwashes and combs, and an attendant who sat on a stool in the corner. From a speaker in the ceiling, "Volare" was discreetly piped in. Meredith and Ann stood in front of the wall of sinks and the huge mirror, and fought. Their words came freely in here; there were no other customers, and somehow the attendant was as unmoving and neutral as a piece of statuary. They could say anything in front of her, and their voices grew louder.

"You have to turn everything into a confrontation," said Meredith. "You're such a goddamn exhibitionist; all you need is a raincoat. Everything has to be aired in public. No wonder Lisa couldn't take it."

"Excuse me?" said Ann. "Suddenly I'm the only one she couldn't take? What about you? What about your nonstop complaining? You're Miss PMS of 1993, and it drove Lisa right over the edge."

"This goes way, way back, doesn't it?" said Meredith. "We were never made to be friends. We weren't even made to have anything to do with each other. The fact that we do is just this freakish little thing about us, like two people who meet when they're trapped in an elevator."

"So get out of the elevator," said Ann.

"I will," said Meredith.

"Good," said Ann. "And go back to your birthday party. I'm sure they're just dying to hear more wacky public TV stories."

"What is it with you?" Meredith asked in a quiet voice. "You just can't be nice to me. Is it a genetic flaw, like the Bad Seed?"

"Meredith, can't you take responsibility for anything?" asked Ann. "We have fucked this thing up together. It's not just me. It's not just you. It's this horrible combination."

"If Lisa was here, she'd make it okay," said Meredith. "She'd do something really corny, like have us look at ourselves in the mirror, and she'd say, 'Do you guys see what you're doing?'"

As if rehearsed, they turned to look at themselves in the mirror. They were both red in the face, overheated, a bit absurd. Ann started to smile. This was about to be a moment of *rapprochement,* but suddenly Meredith couldn't resist peering closer and examining her chin. "Oh great," she said, "you've made me all blotchy. Just what I need. I have to be on camera in the morning."

Ann pulled away, furious again. "Is everything about *you,* Meredith?" she asked. "Everything? Maybe we can find something that isn't. How about the Versailles Treaty. You didn't have anything to do with that, did you?"

"If I piss you off so much, Ann," Meredith said, "then why do you bother?"

"I wish I knew," said Ann. Meredith began to rinse off her face. At the sink beside her, Ann washed her hands.

"I don't even know why I thought we could get along," said Meredith. "This friendship renaissance has been such bullshit. All the phone calls, the pedicures—and by the way, your heels are really in bad shape—all the fake female-bonding. Just because Lisa isn't here. She's the one we want. It's pointless to keep it up. I don't need to take this shit anymore."

"I don't either," said Ann in a sour voice. "I'm going home." At that moment, the bathroom attendant suddenly sprang to life and grimly handed each of them a paper towel. Ann reached into her purse and dug up a tip, which she placed in the dish on the counter. Meredith peered critically at the tip, and opened her mouth to object. "Don't say a word," Ann warned, and Meredith didn't.

When the weather changed, Dale and Meredith took a T'ai Chi class together in the park. They wore similar robes and stood in the grass, moving their arms and legs in synchrony as if in a sluggish underwater ballet. They did everything together, in fact, and they spent every night in one or the other's apartment. It had all happened quickly and naturally, and Meredith felt that even if she was still friends with Ann or Lisa, she probably wouldn't have much time for them anyway, so it really didn't matter that none of them spoke anymore.

A couple of Dale's friends came to his apartment for dinner one night, husband and wife law professors who were lively and appealing. The woman took Meredith aside during coffee and tried to get to know her. At the end of the evening they all had a vague discussion about renting a house in Tuscany the following summer. "I've always wanted to go to Tuscany," Meredith heard herself saying, as though it were true. She had, in fact, always been interested in Italy, but her knowledge of Tuscany itself extended only as far as the fat loaves of Tuscan bread that she sometimes bought at Zabar's. Still, the idea of it sounded good, and this was what young couples did: they dreamed, they planned. As they said goodnight at the door, everyone felt giddy and close and excited. Meredith and Dale lay in bed that night, trying to speak a few words of Italian. "Pronto," he said, rolling the "r."

"Capezio's," she said. "Mastroianni."

Every morning, they put on jogging clothes and sweat bands and went running together in the park. Since she had been involved with Dale, Meredith's body had become tighter and stronger than ever; she had a fantasy that if Lisa or Ann saw her now, they would barely recognize her. She kept thinking she would come across one of them somewhere: in the park, at the movies, at Bloomingdale's. But the city was too big for that; it swept you into different corners, it taught you to walk quickly, and not make eye contact on the street.

The first Monday of the month was approaching. Even though the date was now meaningless, Meredith couldn't help but think about it constantly. "I know that Lisa won't be at the Lucky Wok," she told Dale one night in bed. "She said she's never going to set foot in there as long as she lives. But do you think Ann might be there? After all, we didn't officially cancel the next dinner."

"Come on," said Dale. "After that fight you had in the ladies' room? You should have heard yourselves. The acoustics were amazing."

She knew he was right, and they made plans to stay in on Monday night and order a pizza. But still Meredith wasn't convinced. She worried about it all weekend, and by the time Monday night arrived, she told Dale that he would probably think she was being obsessive, but she simply had to go to the Lucky Wok and make sure that Ann wasn't waiting for her.

* * *

The Lucky Wok was crowded when Meredith walked in. "Hello!" sang out the owner. "You are the first one tonight!" He showed Meredith to the usual table.

"Actually," Meredith said, "it's just going to be two of us tonight. Or maybe just me. I'm really not sure."

She sat at the table and waited. The door kept swinging open, bringing in new clusters of people. Customers stood in the doorway and looked around the restaurant until they found their friends. Coats were removed, cheeks were kissed, waiters carried trays high in the air. It was getting late. Meredith sipped her water and picked up her menu, idly glancing at it. She had long ago memorized everything that was printed here in black and red type. The dishes were as familiar as her own name by now. Some of them had odd names; one was called "shrimp versus chicken," as though poultry and seafood had some age-old, legendary rivalry.

Meredith was sitting alone reading the menu and wondering whether she should give up and leave, when suddenly a waiter came striding up to her table, holding a flaming platter aloft. A few people stopped to look at the dramatic presentation as the dish was placed in front of Meredith.

"Sizzling ginger chicken," said the waiter. "With compliments."

"Oh God," said Meredith. "I do not believe this. Look, this is not a good night. I don't even think I'm staying; my friend hasn't arrived, and I was about to leave. I won't be able to eat this. Please tell whoever sent it that I appreciate it and everything, but I really have to send it back."

"The customer says you are a very lovely lady," the waiter persisted.

"All right," said Meredith. She sighed. "Who is it?" The waiter pointed to the front of the room. Meredith turned and looked, and there was Ann, standing by the cash register, her coat still on, smirking in that familiar way. They just looked at each other for a very long moment, and then Ann walked over to the table to help Meredith put out the flames.

Dinner was as awkward and tentative as a blind date. Ann talked about her job with Evan Bright, and told clever stories about what it was like being an agent. Meredith talked about Dale, and how they were even thinking about marriage. "That's wonderful," Ann and Meredith said to each other when they finished up their little set-pieces about their lives.

But it wasn't working; they couldn't find a way to talk. It was so uncomfortable without Lisa, so preposterous. Meredith had always imagined that the three of them would know each other until they died. They would grow old together, three women who had outlasted their men, three widows who would take year-long cruises around the world, eating everything they pleased—Napoleons, blackout cake, pastas bathed in cream sauce—and then when they returned home, they would open up a small business: an adorable yet elegant restaurant, or an exclusive boutique. As old age grabbed them by the heart or the lungs or, like so many women, by their snappable, calcium-leeched bones, Lisa would be their own personal doctor, taking pulses, writing prescriptions, tapping knees. Their grown children would occasionally drop by: big, strapping young men and their wives, or duty-bound daughters and their mild husbands. Meredith, Lisa, and

Ann would start to shrink, like old people often did, their bodies curling up like shrimp thrown into boiling water. They would die off, one by one, and attend each other's funerals, and the one who died last would feel an emptiness in her life unlike anything she had ever experienced, an emptiness that went beyond even the terrible pain of widowhood. They had known each other forever, and it all came down to this! They had gone from girls to women to old women to very old women, and now the whole thing was coming to an end, and there was so much they still wanted to do. *It's not fair,* they would cry, as death separated them. *We're MerLisAn. We're supposed to be together forever!*

But it wouldn't even come to that. They wouldn't see each other get old, they wouldn't get to follow it through, because they simply weren't friends anymore. "Oh God, Ann," Meredith suddenly said in the Chinese restaurant, "I can't believe this. We've put all these years into it, and now: nothing. You know, I thought I was over Lisa, but I think about her all the time. I keep wondering what she's doing, and whether she and Eric are really getting a divorce. I even wonder about Joshua, whether he has more hair on his head by now, or whether he's going to spend his life looking like Henry, that weird kid in the comic strip. I want to know these things, you know? I feel like I have a right to know them." Meredith suddenly felt as though she might cry. She fumbled in her pocketbook for a tissue.

"Meredith," said Ann, "please don't cry. Not again. I want to come back to this restaurant, and they already think we're weird enough, between your crying fits, and my sending you the ginger chicken."

Meredith wiped at her eyes and sat up straighter. "All

right, I'll try to control myself," she said.

"For what it's worth," said Ann, "I'm sick about it too. I've been fighting with Emily all the time, I have a lot of trouble sleeping, and I have a new job that terrifies me. I want to see Lisa, I just want to *talk* to her. That's the only thing that would make me feel better." She tapped a chopstick lightly against her plate. "You know what?" she said suddenly. "I think we should go there. Tonight."

"There? Where?" asked Meredith.

"Lisa's apartment," said Ann.

"You mean, just show up?" said Meredith. "Are you crazy?"

"An ambush," said Ann. "I see no other way."

Quickly, they finished their dinner, ignoring the plate of pineapple cubes that was placed before them, and then they found themselves outside in the darkening evening, walking quickly in the direction of Lisa's building.

"What are we doing?" Meredith asked, as they turned the corner and the green awning came into view.

"I have no idea," said Ann. And then they went inside.

Fourteen

Since Eric was gone and Meredith and Ann had been banished, Lisa and the baby had become constant companions. She looked to him for conversation, for response, for entertainment, and after a while, as though comprehending the depth of his mother's need, his round face actually seemed to assume a variety of intelligent, adult expressions. He raised his eyebrows, he stroked his chin, he appeared to listen like a social worker. When she came home from the hospital each day, she would order takeout, and they would spend a quiet evening together. Sometimes, as she placed him in his crib and wound up his mobile and flicked on the moon nightlight that cast a yellowish haze over Joshua's corner of the living room, Lisa almost thought she was happy. But later, when he was asleep and she was alone with her thoughts, she remembered how awful she felt, and how much she wanted everyone to come back.

Eric called her every night, describing life in Wilmington, telling her he was very confused about what he should do. He wasn't happy working for his uncles, but he couldn't imagine being happy anywhere. His eight weeks were almost up, and he would be home in a few days, and they would have to decide whether they would separate or not. At work, Lisa's patients seemed older and more desperate than ever, a spooky reminder of the fact that Lisa had better have fun now, while she was young.

She began slipping on the job. Just the other day she had spent an hour trying to find a vein in an old man who screamed so much that nurses kept popping their heads in the door to make sure everything was okay. The more the man screamed, the more clumsy Lisa became, and pretty soon his screaming was totally justified, and she didn't know when to stop, she just kept poking dully at his poor white arm until the head nurse came in, sized up the situation, and took over. Within moments, the nurse had found a usable vein, and the man was quiet. When Lisa came back later to check up on him, he shouted, "Don't come near me!" and rolled over in his bed to face the wall. Lisa simply burst into tears and left the room. She went into the doctors' lounge and actually bummed a Kool off a gastroenterologist—she, who hadn't smoked a cigarette since adolescence, and only then because Meredith smoked. Now Lisa sat in the lounge on the ugly orange plastic couch, and closed her eyes and smoked, feeling the fumes enter her body and start to pollute her. She wasn't breastfeeding anymore; she could do what she liked. She didn't have a husband, so there was no one to complain about the smell of smoke on her hair and clothes. She wasn't friends with Meredith and Ann anymore, either, so there was no one to mock her for this unlikely act, no one to say, as Ann probably would, "I am shocked. *Shocked*."

Lisa often wondered what Meredith and Ann were doing. Whenever they had called her answering machine and she had been home, she had actually gotten up from her chair and gone right over to the machine, listening as they left a message, as though to be near them in some way. But she couldn't stop feeling furious at them, and if she gave in and picked up the telephone when they called, this would be what they expected from her. Lisa the Nice, Lisa the Endlessly Forgiving Fountain of Love and Warmth. Lisa, to whom they could go for a dose of comfort and reassurance whenever they fucked up in the same dumb ways they always did.

But now, incredibly, they were back. The doorman had waved them upstairs without ringing, and now here they were, on the other side of her triple-locked door. Lisa had been carrying Joshua to his crib when she heard feverish whispering in the hall. She went and stood unmoving by the door, holding the baby.

"You ring it!" she heard, and she realized it was Meredith's voice.

"No, you!"

"She's not going to know who rang."

"She'll know."

Lisa peered through the peephole, and there she saw Meredith and Ann, their convex faces too close to the door so that they looked like grotesques with big, fleshy noses and chins. Lisa felt her heart start to race.

"Lisa? It's us," said Meredith. "Can we come in?" But Lisa couldn't answer.

"Dr. Vopilska to Emergency!" called Ann. "Dr. Vopilska to Emergency! There are two Siamese twins here who need to be separated!"

Lisa leaned against her side of the door, repositioning

the baby, who tugged at her earrings. "Lisa," said Meredith, "we're just going to park ourselves here until you open up. We will not be moved."

Fine, she thought. *Stay there, I am not letting you in. I am not going to be a fucking pushover.* From the hallway, they begin to hum "We Shall Overcome," and then Ann started to sing the song with a new set of lyrics, and soon Meredith joined in. "Please open the door," they sang. "Please open the door / Please open the door / Li-sa-a-a-a / Oh deep in my heart / I do believe / That you'll open the door, Lisa . . ."

Lisa still couldn't bring herself to say or do anything, so they began a second verse: "We don't hate your hu-us-band / We don't hate your hu-us-band /We don't hate your husband / Li-sa-a-a-a / Oh deep in your heart / you do believe / that we don't hate your husband, Lisa."

When they finished singing, there was total stillness from the other side of the door, as though they were both holding their breath to see how she would respond. She had hated them up until this minute, had been certain they would never again speak, but now, hearing these voices that were as familiar and wrenching as her own baby's cry in the night, she could not resist. Being a mother has made me into a sap, she thought, as she quickly unlocked all three locks and opened the door.

There they were, standing side by side and looking slightly different than she had remembered. Ann had a new haircut, and Meredith seemed changed, too, somehow calmer and glossier than ever. Lisa stood facing them, the baby on her hip, and behind her the apartment was a jumble of books and clothes and squeak toys, which had all collected into a wild overgrowth since Eric had left. "Yes?" Lisa said coldly.

"Ann rang the bell," said Meredith.

"Lisa," said Ann, "I just want to tell you something. We've known each other too long for this. You can't just disappear. You want to be like Amelia Earhart? You want to be like Judge Crater? You want to be like . . . Barbara? Just slip away forever and hope that after a while it won't matter? Well, it does. I mean, there are always going to be people who float in and out of your life, and you don't see them for years, and then they just show up again. Or sometimes they never show up, and you live the rest of your life without them, wondering what happened, and whatever became of them. Is that what you want? You want to just float away? Well, I won't let you." She paused, but Lisa didn't say anything. "Come on, Lisa," said Ann, "we *know* each other. You can't just disappear; we belong together. Tell me, what else is there in life, what else is as important as your friends? I really want to know."

Of course Ann spoke beautifully. Of course Lisa was moved. Of course she wanted nothing more than to be rescued, swept away from this crowded apartment and the scant remains of her marriage, but it seemed too easy to just cave in to this thing called friendship, simply because it had been there forever.

"We're getting through to you," said Ann. "I see tears in those eyes. Yes, the ice is breaking. You're coming back to us, Lisa. You're coming back!"

"Jesus, she's not in a coma, Ann," said Meredith.

"Can't I say it the way I want to?" asked Ann, and she and Meredith gave each other withering looks. It was amazing how quickly those two could snipe at each other, Lisa thought, and somehow this fact brought her back to the middle of this friendship, where they were the warriors and she was the peacemaker, and nothing ever changed.

"Just come inside already," said Lisa flatly. Once inside, they all paused for a moment, looking to Lisa for a cue, unsure of what was going to happen next. Then, despite herself, Lisa smiled. Ann and Meredith reached out toward her, and they were all hugging and chattering, the baby wedged in the middle.

"So," said Lisa, as someone closed the door, "what did I miss?"

One year later, on the wide stone terrace of a country club on the outskirts of Magatuck, Meredith Grey married Dale Sanger. No one at the wedding seemed surprised; this marriage had an air of inevitability about it, which everyone accepted. "Friend of the bride or the groom?" wedding guests cheerfully asked each other as they mingled during cocktails after the ceremony, but the answer hardly mattered. To an astonishing degree, Meredith and Dale had become one unified being, a fashionable two-backed beast, a collection of wonderful fabrics, legendary givers of good dinner parties, all poise and grace. Everyone envied them and surely spoke against them from time to time in small, sniping ways. But what was the worst you could say about such a couple? You could say that the woman was superficial, and that the man was a bit vague for his own good. But still you wanted to be near them, to eat their dinners and listen to their conversation, and of course you wanted to be there when they finally got married.

At the reception, Meredith and Ann walked through the room arm in arm, stark opposites in black and white, stopping at tables to chat like the President and the First Lady at a state dinner. Over at table #1, Lisa sat looking out across the polished dance floor, where a few older couples danced and Eric twirled Joshua around while the band played a melody that was so soft and bland it could have been anything. Eric had shaved off his beard—perhaps to symbolize change in his marriage to Lisa, perhaps because it was beginning to itch that summer. What Lisa had feared all along was true: he had no real chin to speak of, although he was still a handsome man. Ann sat across the table, between David Marcus and a tall, athletic woman, a lesbian friend of Dale's from law school, named Ingrid. Five months earlier, Emily had broken up with Ann, announcing one night that she had met another woman at a Queer Nation meeting—a Japanese performance artist named Kiko—and that they had fallen in love. Ann had sobbed and tried to throw Emily's own words back at her: *You said lesbian couples stay together forever!* she had cried, but Emily only muttered embarrassed apologies and made plans to leave. Ever since then, various friends had been trying to fix Ann up with someone new. She had gone out on awkward dates with a few different women, and had been to bed a couple more times with David, but she had recently told Lisa that she had no idea whether she wanted to end up with a man or a woman.

How did anyone choose anyone? Lisa wondered. Even if you had narrowed the field to men, it was hard to know if you had made the right decision. Lisa often wondered if she should have taken Eric back when he came home at the end of his eight weeks at his uncles' dermatology practice; she still wasn't sure of how they had made their peace. Eric hadn't liked life in Delaware; his uncles were surprisingly old-fashioned in their methodology; they paid little attention to the new dermatological advances, and Eric couldn't see staying there and making a life with them. He missed his life in New York; he missed his wife and son. He begged Lisa to let him return, and at first she was resistant, but gradually he wore her resistance down, and they ended up in bed. Over the following weeks, he and Lisa had tried to talk about what had gone wrong in their marriage, but the conversation never reached a *Scenes from a Marriage* type of intensity or length, because in the middle Joshua always seemed to need a bottle, or a new diaper, and the business of being parents inevitably eclipsed everything else.

Now they lived in a bigger apartment with an actual bedroom for the baby, and Eric had joined a group practice with two other young, nervous dermatologists, who advertised only in newspapers, and never on subways. Life was not exciting in the Vopilska-Zinn household, but it wasn't terrible, either, and Lisa realized that she finally did have everyone around her, the way she had always thought she wanted.

At some point during Meredith's wedding, after all the sentimental toasts were over, and the cake had been distributed, when the party was calm and the light through the tall windows was growing weak, Meredith, Lisa, and Ann went back outside to the terrace. Meredith hiked up her dress and they sat on the stone ledge together, looking out over the grass, and the turnpike in the distance, where they used to walk.

"Is this supposed to be fun?" Meredith asked. "Lisa, did you have fun at your wedding?"

"No," said Lisa.

"Maybe this is one of life's big, dumb mistakes," said Meredith.

"Meredith, what is wrong with you?" Lisa asked. "Dale is the catch of the century, can't you see that?"

"I know he is," said Meredith, miserably. "And we're very happy together, really. I never get sick of him, and that's a first for me. You know, we even finished reading *Middlemarch*. It ends in such a great way." She struggled to quote the final line of the book: *"But the effect of her being on those around her was . . ."* Here she faltered. "Yadda yadda," she continued. "And then George Eliot goes on to say something about how the good of the world is dependent on what she calls 'unhistoric acts,' and how the fact that things really aren't so bad is sort of because of all those people 'who lived hidden lives, and *rest in unvisited tombs.*'"

They were all silent for a moment, then Lisa said, "That's beautiful, Meredith. I don't know what it means, exactly, but it's beautiful."

"We're going to start reading *Buddenbrooks* on our honeymoon," said Meredith. "We *are* happy, but how do you ever know that it will last? How do you know that it won't turn into a big tragedy later on?"

"I guess you can't know that," said Lisa.

"What about all that trouble that you and Eric had?" Meredith asked. "I know things are a little better now, but are you ever sorry that you got married? Do you ever feel little twinges of regret?"

"Oh, sure," said Lisa. "I have fantasies. What it would be like if we weren't married. Or if we'd gotten a divorce, like I thought we would. You probably won't understand this, but I know Eric the way I know things I learned in medical school. The way I know the names of all the bones of the body. Not just the big ones, but all the weird little ones, too. Like the bones of the ear."

"I have bones in my ear?" said Ann. "I never knew that."

"Yeah, three of them," said Lisa. "The malleus, the incus, and the stapes."

"Wow," said Ann. She reached up and experimentally bent the top of her own ear.

"I used to stay up all night memorizing these things," said Lisa. "I'd picture the way they looked, and learn every little thing about them. Finally they stuck. And they're with me forever." She shrugged. "And so is Eric," she added lightly.

"I thought I was going to be with Emily forever," said Ann. "It never occurred to me that even in a lesbian relationship I could be cheated on."

"If you want to know the truth," said Meredith, "I was never really crazy about Emily."

"Why," said Ann, "because of her sexuality?"

"No, because of her personality," said Meredith. "She was so bossy."

"Well, that's a laugh, coming from you," said Ann.

"Are you implying that I'm bossy?"

"If that's what you infer," said Ann.

"Stop it, both of you," said Lisa. "I can't believe you're doing this. It's your wedding, Meredith. So act sweet and virginal for a change."

From behind them there came a tapping on the window. They turned and saw Dale beckoning Meredith inside. "I should go in," she said. "More photo ops, probably."

"Will you be okay?" Lisa asked her.

"God, I hope so," said Meredith.

"Then let's go," said Ann. They walked across the terrace, Meredith's train trailing behind her, while Ann and Lisa struggled to keep it from touching the ground.

Later, the band played a dull medley of rock songs from the 70s, and a few diehards were still dancing. Eric had gone to change Joshua's diaper in the empty banquet room next door, lying him down on a tablecloth spread out over the gold-flocked carpeting. Dale was off in a corner with a couple of his law school friends, smoking big cigars like satisfied businessmen. Meredith, Lisa, and Ann stood at the side of the room, just watching. It was almost time to go.

"Can't they play anything good?" asked Ann. "This music is like the easy listenin' station at my gynecologist's."

"Like what?" asked Meredith. "What would be good?"

"I don't know," said Ann. "But I'm going to ask them to play something. I haven't made a single request all day."

Meredith and Lisa looked at each and shrugged as Ann approached the young, thick-bodied lead singer between songs. Curious, they followed her up to the band platform. "Excuse me," they heard her say, "do you take requests?"

"Yeah, sure," the singer answered. "What do you want, Beatles? Nostalgia is very big these days."

"No," said Ann. "Do you know 'The MerLisAn Song'?"

"The what?" he asked.

Meredith and Lisa started to laugh. "Ann!" Lisa hissed. "What are you doing?"

"You might know it under its former name," Ann persisted. " 'The Mer*Ba*LisAn song.' "

"Yeah, and who supposedly recorded it?" asked the man.

"Fleetwood Mac," she said.

Now all three women began to laugh, and the singer shook his head. "Sorry, girls," he said. "I can't help you." He turned away and the band played something else slow and quiet.

"Well," said Ann, "we'll show you how it goes." She beckoned Lisa and Meredith over toward an available corner of the dance floor.

"You're crazy," said Lisa.

"Come on," said Ann. "Let's do it. No one's looking."

"This is my wedding," said Meredith. "Dale will think I'm psychotic. He'll have the marriage annulled." She looked around at the tired relatives, the waiters clearing tables, her new husband off somewhere in a billow of fragrant male smoke. "Oh," said Meredith, "what the fuck." Then she shrugged and impulsively reached out her arms to Lisa and Ann. They linked hands and quietly, self-consciously, started to sing.

"I'm Meredith!" the song began.

"I'm Lisa!"

"Hmm-hmm-hmm!"

"I'm Ann!"

"Listen very closely and we'll tell you our plan / We're friends from the soul and we're friends from the heart / We're friends forever and we're never gonna part / Mer*hmm*LisAn, Mer*hmm*LisAn / Friends forever, Mer-*hmm*LisAn . . ."

A couple of Meredith's aunts applauded, and a few other guests shook their heads. The three of them spun in their circle and they sang, and suddenly, to her surprise, Lisa began to think about their long-lost friend Barbara. Barbara Krell, who had once been one of them, whose name had appeared in their song. Barbara, who had been swallowed up by Cincinnati as a child, and was never retrieved.

With a new urgency, Lisa now wondered where Barbara was, and what she did for a living, and whether she had ever been in love. Lisa wanted to tell Barbara that she and Meredith and Ann had actually made it in one piece. Three pieces, actually. Meredith and Ann were never going to be great friends. But they had made it, and that was all that mattered. Lisa wanted someone to notice. So Barbara, she thought, as they began another chorus of this ridiculous and heartbreaking song: wherever you are, this is for you.